CU01083942

Whisper

Of

Ghosts

Irene Howarth

Irene Howarth

Cover image by Raggedstone/Shutterstock

This book is a work of fiction. Names, characters, places, and incidents either are products of the author's imagination or are used fictitiously. Any resemblance to actual persons, living or dead, events, or locales is entirely coincidental.

Printed in the United Kingdom
First Printing August 2024
ISBN 979-8-3232678-2-8

Especially for David and Emily

Family and friends for the support and encouragement
in writing my debut novel

A special mention to Amy. Thanks for the fresh eyes!

Best wishes, x

Irene Howarth

THE PAST

CHAPTER 1

'Okay,' Spud thought, 'I'm not that tired, but I am tired.' He flicked open his eyes against the encroaching sleep.

The shouting coming from downstairs was nothing new to him. He was used to it, his parents shouting and screaming at each other.

It made his head hurt.

Now, he was nearly ten and could understand the words they yelled. It upset him.

Spud could feel the tears building up in his tired eyes. Frustrated, he pulled the pillow from under him and covered his head to drown out the noise from below. It helped a little, but not much. He closed his eyes, and sleep finally took him over.

Rose looked at Seth, and with a sigh, she pulled out a chair and sat at the kitchen table. She held her head for a few seconds and then stared up at her husband, who leaned against the kitchen sink, arms folded, and glared at her.

'Well.' he snarled. 'Not got a smart answer this time. Huh?'

Rose sighed again. 'Seth, I'm tired of all of this.' She motioned around the kitchen.

'What's wrong with all of this?' he mocked her. 'It's fantastic.'

'It might be for you. All this was your parents. None of it is mine.'

Seth leaned on the table, hands splayed and stared menacingly into Rose's eyes. 'Nope. It's all mine.'

Before she knew it, she blurted out. 'And Eric's'

She heard for her lack of thought before she felt the slap across her face.

'Don't you mention that piece of shit's name in this house. EVER.'

Holding onto her face, Rose sobbed. 'Seth, he's your brother.'

Seth slammed his fists onto the table. 'I don't care if I ever see him again.' His calm voice contradicted his red face and the vein that throbbed at his temple.

Startled, Rose knew she had better get out of his way. Fast.

She dashed out of the kitchen, ran up the stairs and slammed her bedroom door.

Seth took a deep breath, then poured himself a glass of water. He stared out of the kitchen window while he gulped the water down.

His shaking began to subside, and he felt control coming over him.

'Eric, Eric, Eric.' He muttered. 'You sneaky bastard.'

He stared at the empty glass in his hand and contemplated smashing it into the sink. Instead, he gently placed it on the draining board.

The bare staircase creaked as he slowly made his way to the bedroom. He smiled at the thought of Rose lying in bed, hoping he would leave her alone tonight.

No chance, Seth scoffed.

CHAPTER 2

Rose had a lot to think about. Last night was the last straw. When she'd heard him creaking up the bare stairs, her only thought was for Michael, or Spud, as Seth called him. For all his bravado, Seth went straight to sleep.

It was about time she made the most of her situation and stood up for herself, not just shouting and trying to get her point across to Seth, but actually doing something about it.

First, she was going to start with the bare staircase. This was her home, too, and there was no way, from now on, she would let Seth intimidate her. After all, they were a married couple, supposed to support and love each other, right?

But no matter how hard she tried to think positively about her marriage to Seth, Rose couldn't.

The memories of the house would not leave her alone. And that morning, while she put the washing out on a rare, dry, sunny day, Rose began to cry. 'Stop it.' she stammered and wiped her tears away.

From the garden, Rose could see into the kitchen—a place she hated. She closed her eyes against the sun, but a vision came to her, a vision she wanted to keep hidden at the back of her mind. But every day she stayed in this house, it crushed her soul.

From the moment Seth had laid his hands on her, she knew there was no going back.

Back to the love of her life. Back to the one person who had really loved her.

The memories of that night would haunt her for the rest of her life.

'Seth, what are you doing? Please don't do that.' She begged when he'd put his hand up her dress.

'Come on, Rose, I love you. It's what people in love do, right?'

Rose tried to tug his hand away. 'Stop it, now.'

Suddenly, Seth hauled her onto the kitchen table and pinned her down. She pushed against him, but he was stronger.

Rose tried not to cry as his breathing in her ear became deeper and louder. She could feel him pushing inside her faster and faster.

Then he was done.

Seth pushed himself off her and pulled up his trousers.

'Don't lie there exposing yourself. Go clean yourself up before my parents come back.'

Rose pulled her dress down and gingerly got off the table. The tears came as she locked herself in the toilet. She hurt and never felt so humiliated.

'Eric.' she stammered. 'I'm sorry.'

Rose didn't want to tell Seth. She knew it would be the worst thing she could do. But when she began to show, she had to.

That was the end for Rose. There was no going back to her true love. Eric wouldn't take seconds.

The prospect of marriage to Seth horrified Rose, but her angry and humiliated father would have it no other way.

At the altar, she wondered if Eric would stand up and be a man. Maybe he would have if he'd known the truth had he been there.

But here she was, stuck in a marriage she never wanted. The only thing keeping her going was Michael. As soon as he was born, she promised him she would never leave him.

Never.

A few days later, Rose couldn't wait for Micheal to come home from school, and as soon as he stepped foot into the house, she ambushed him. 'Look, Michael, what do you think?' she guided a stumped Spud toward the stairs. 'How much better does that look?'

Spud looked from the red swirly stair carpet to his mother's smiling face. 'It looks nice.'

Rose hugged him. 'Isn't it just? And what a difference it'll make come the cold weather.'

Unfortunately, her enthusiasm wasn't to last.

CHAPTER 3

Seth stood at the bottom of the stairs and listened hard, trying to hear any noise from Spud's bedroom.

He knew Spud would often creep to the top of the landing, poke his head over the handrail and listen to him and his mother argue. Well, this time was going to be the last.

Tonight was going to be different. This time, Rose, his wife of ten years, would respect him.

In the kitchen, Seth waited for Rose to come downstairs. 'We need to talk,' Seth demanded as soon as she entered the kitchen.

'What now, Seth?' Rose reluctantly sat at the kitchen table opposite him.

'Don't use that tone with me. I'm sick of it.'

'And I'm sick of you, Seth. What do you want to talk to me about? Sorry, moan about, more like it.'

She felt her brain was a pinball, bouncing from side to side as the shock of Seth's slap receded.

'I've had enough of you.' Suddenly, his face was so close to hers that Rose could feel his spittle on her face, and that awful night came flooding back to her.

Without hesitation, Rose shot out of her chair, grabbed one of the kitchen knives drying on the drainer, and jabbed it at Seth.

'You get away from me, Seth. I'll use it.' She sobbed. 'Leave, leave me and Michael. Go stay with one of your sluts you can control because you ain't going to control me or Michael no more, Seth. I'm done.'

'Oh, sweet thing. How sexy you sound. Come on, let's go make another baby right now, right here.' He sneaked a look down at the table. 'Right where we made Spud.' He laughed at her.

Rose had to suppress a smirk. If only he knew he could never produce a son like Michael.

'Stop calling him that. His name is Michael. He's only ten years old, and it upsets him.'

'He's a little kid, and I'll call him whatever name I want.'

'Seth, please.' Rose held the knife up, ready to bring it down.

'I suggest you put the knife down, Rose, unless you plan to use it.'

Seth was getting too close, and her breath came shorter and faster. 'Seth, I don't want to use the knife, but I will.' She glanced at the knife in her hand and noticed it was shaking, her hand was shaking, and her whole body was shaking.

'Give it to me.'

Seth was so close that Rose felt the heat of his anger.

'Seth, please. I don't want to fight anymore.'

'Don't worry, sweetheart, you won't.'

Before she knew it, Seth grabbed her arm and yanked the knife from her hand so quickly she didn't have time to let go of it.

Rose screamed and stared at the blood dripping onto the floor.

In shock, she stammered. 'Seth, I'm bleeding.' She stared at him, her hand out toward him, expecting he would help her.

11

'Oh, that's a shame.' Seth grinned at her. With the knife in one hand, he began to unzip his trousers with the other.

Rose knew what was coming next. Her heart was pounding, and without thinking, she raced past him and headed to the front door.

Ignoring the agonising pain in her right hand, she fumbled with the lock and threw the door open.

The night waited for her.

Surprised at her hesitation, not sure whether to take the step over the threshold, she looked back over her shoulder, up at Michael's closed bedroom door.

What if she left? What if she just ran away from the man in the kitchen with a knife in his hand?

What about her promise to Michael as she held him in her arms moments after he was born?

Her hands clung to the door frame. The relentless rain fell, blurring Rose's vision as she tried to scan the darkness in front of her. A fear clenched her heart.

But she knew she had to go.

She glanced at Seth, who impatiently tapped the knife against his leg as if waiting for her to come back inside, close the door, and give herself up to him after begging for his forgiveness.

Rose let go of the doorframe. Her left foot edged over the doorstep, followed by her right foot.

Run! Run! Her head screamed.

The clatter of the knife on the kitchen floor spurred her on.

Now!

Rose felt like her legs belonged to someone else as if she were watching another person take the first steps to freedom. 'I can make it,' a voice in her head urged. Her legs moved faster, and the wind and rain that pelted her face went unnoticed.

She ran barefoot across the lawn, almost slipping on the wet grass. In the distance, the light of neighbours was a beacon of hope. But behind her, she could hear Seth's guttural, heavy breathing and the squelching of his boots on the soaked grass getting closer and closer.

Rose screamed as Seth grabbed a chunk of her long hair and pulled her backwards. She collapsed on the grass, gasping for breath.

Seth's grip on her hair intensified the pain, leaving her disorientated.

For a few seconds, she couldn't speak. Then, the blurred image of Seth straddling her came into clear view.

'Where do you think you're going?' he yelled over the sound of the rain and the wind.

'Let go of me, Seth.' She screamed in his face.

Seth grabbed her wrists, hauled her to her feet, and dragged her away from the house.

'Where are you taking me?' she gasped.

'Somewhere where you'll never bother me again.' Seth slapped his hand over her mouth.

Rose struggled to breathe as the darkness came over her and she flayed at Seth, pulling at his hair and scratching at his face and hands.

But he didn't stop. He continued to drag her along the dimly lit path and up the slight incline toward the far corner of the field, which led to only one place.

The woods.

The woods that surrounded Blyneath House.

Rose struggled harder.

THE PRESENT

CHAPTER 4

As soon as Freya opened the door to her apartment, an excited Arthur greeted her. She bent to hug him, then gently closed the door behind her. 'Come on, Arthur, I'll feed you.' While she watched her brown spaniel scoff at his food, she leaned against the cupboards, closed her eyes, and inhaled deeply. When she opened her eyes again, tears fell.

Freya wiped her face. 'Not again.' She whispered into the emptiness.

She took off her coat and hung it on the coat rack along with her handbag, then went into the lounge, where she headed for the bay window, followed by Arthur, who jumped up on her lap.

Freya liked to sit on the cushioned bay window seat and watch the world go by. Across the road, she watched as children, out of school but still in school uniforms, played football, hung upside down on the bars, or swung too high on the wooden swings (or so Freya thought).

She smiled wistfully.

The bang of the front door closing startled her. Arthur jumped from her lap and headed for his basket in the corner of the room.

'Freya.' An anxious voice filled the air.

'In here.' she sounded more cheerful than she felt.

Freya forced a smile as her husband gingerly entered the room, but as soon as he smiled back, she couldn't hold it together any longer, and the tears came again.

Owen rushed to her and took hold of her. 'I'm so sorry, Freya.' He held onto her until her tears subsided. 'It'll be okay, I promise.' He whispered in her ear.

Freya pushed him away. 'I can't do this anymore, Owen. It hurts every time.'

Owen tried to take hold of her hand.

'No, don't. I've had enough.' She shoved his hand away. 'I'm done. I can't go through this again. It's all right for you. I'm the one going through IVF. It hurts Owen. My body can't take it anymore.'

'Okay, I understand that, but maybe, just, well, why don't we just give all this IVF a miss? Have a break for a few months. Let you get your strength back.' He smiled at his wife, who, he thought, did look tired, hurt, and defeated.

'I guess, but I'm not promising just a few months. I need more time than that.'

Owen nodded and watched her as she left the room. He turned and looked out of the bay window across the road toward the playground at the children playing. Brushing his hands through his pepper-coloured hair, he wondered if his age might have something to do with them not getting pregnant again.

Owen and Freya married as soon as she found out she was pregnant. They were both ecstatic but surprised. Things had happened so quickly.

But he loved her and thought, now that he was heading for the wrong side of forty, he would take this opportunity, this gift, to have Freya, who was almost 15 years his junior, and have a family.

It would be a big adjustment for him. He would have to cut down on his travels, conferences abroad, and the luxury of having whomever he wanted at his beck and call.

He would change for Freya.

Since that first miscarriage, getting pregnant again seemed impossible, and it was getting them both down, Freya more so. It was like she thought her body was giving up on her.

Owen sighed and came away from the window. He heard the shower running. He had enough on his plate as it was, anyway, and if he was being truthful, he was beginning to get exasperated with Freya.

Every day, Owen tried his damnedest to keep smiling against Freya's moods, which could be soul-destroying for him. Her nastiness toward him when she realised she wasn't pregnant interfered with his work and concentration. There was only so much Alan would allow to slip.

The shower stopped.

Not wanting any confrontations, Owen headed to the kitchen and busied himself with making them dinner.

He heard Freya's slippers on the wooden floorboards.

'I'm sorry.' She put her arms around his waist. 'I think it would be a good idea if we had a break, maybe even take a holiday?'

Owen turned to her and kissed her on the cheek. 'I think that is a great idea. I'll have a word with Alan tomorrow. And just because it's the only thing I make with some success, I've made our favourite, Spaghetti Bolognese.'

An hour after dinner, Freya turned to Owen. 'I'm tired. I'm going to have an early night.'

'Shall I come and join you?' Owen winked at her.

Freya hesitated in the doorway and looked down at her feet. 'No, I need a good night's sleep. Thanks for dinner, though; it was great.' She blew Owen a kiss and disappeared.

Owen turned on the TV, kept the volume low, and put his feet up on the coffee table. Some detective show was on, but he wasn't concentrating on it.

Tomorrow was going to be a busy day. The advertising agency had so much work that they needed to hire more staff.

Alan would not be pleased when he told him he was going on holiday.

CHAPTER 5

Owen had to look away as Alan Young sat at his desk and glared at him. 'There is no way you can go on holiday now, Owen. No bloody way. You know we have to keep ahead of our rivals, and you pissing off to some sunnier place will not help.'

'I know, I know, but Alan, you know what Freya's been going through. All this IVF and the miscarriages have taken their toll on her. and me. Come on, just a few days then?'

Alan sighed. 'Okay. But as soon as you get back, I want over 100 per cent from you.'

'You know it. Thanks, Alan, you might have just saved my marriage.'

As Owen left the room, Alan said. 'By the way, Owen, what do you think about developing an internship scheme?'

'Why? I know we need more staff, but who would be their mentor?'

'You leave that with me. I'll sort it for when you get back from your holiday.'

Owen chuckled. 'No wonder you are the CEO, Alan.'

Alan smiled. 'And don't you forget it. Now, go.'

Owen closed the office door behind him and headed for the lift. He wondered how he would cope on this mini holiday with Freya.

He hated not being included in crucial decisions, and introducing an internship was a big decision.

Owen knew he wouldn't relax on holiday and vowed to keep in contact with Alan behind Freya's back. The last thing he wanted was a fight on holiday.

CHAPTER 6

'Mr Lyle, I don't know what to say?'

'Lana, you have an amazing talent well suited to advertising.

I'll never lie to you.'

'Wow.' Lana gazed up into the brown, sexy eyes of her boss and mentor. 'Thank you.'

Owen walked away, leaving Lana in the middle of the vestibule, nervously twisting her hands.

One of the firm's top secretaries walked past her, giving her a pitying look.

Lana looked away and toyed with her long, blond hair. When the secretary was out of sight, she hurried to the ladies' room.

Thankfully, no one else was in the toilets. Lana checked her face in the mirror. 'Perfect, ' she told her reflection. I'm perfect. They're just jealous because Owen Lyle likes me and asked *me* out to dinner.'

Owen and Lana followed the waiter to their table. The waiter pulled out a chair for Lana. 'This place is amazing. Do you eat here a lot?' Lana fiddled with her clothes and hair.

Owen sat opposite her. 'Stop fiddling; you look great.'

'I'm surprised you can see me. It's dark in here.'

'It's called ambience, Lana.'

Owen grinned. 'No. I thought I'd like to try something new. Bit fed up with the posh nosh I normally eat.'.

21

Lana stared at him. 'What, you don't think I'm good enough for posh nosh?'

Owen leaned toward her. 'Of course I do. But do you really want to spend time in the company of obnoxious pratts who think they're the bee's knees? There's enough of them at work.'

'I see.' Lana smiled her sweetest smile.

Owen leaned back in his chair and eyed the young, beautiful intern who had fallen into his lap.

After dinner, they walked hand in hand to the taxi rank, and Owen put Lana in a waiting taxi.

'Can't you come home with me?' her eyes were full of mischief.

'I don't know.' He looked at his watch. 'I guess I could, for a little while.' He smiled and jumped into the taxi.

At Lana's apartment, Owen took off his jacket and tie and placed them on the sofa. He turned to her, held her face in his hands and kissed her

'Are you sure you want to do this?' Owen nuzzled into her neck.

Lana murmured into his kiss. 'Yes.' She gasped. 'Yes, take me, Owen, now.'

He carried Lana to her bedroom and put her down on her feet. Slowly, he undressed her. Owen pulled down her skimpy underwear and kissed her between her legs. He felt her shiver. He made his way down her thighs, kissing every inch until he got to her feet.

Lana let him guide her onto the bed, where she shoved a pink sparkly book onto the floor.

'We won't be disturbed?' he whispered.

'No, this is my place. No one lives here but me.'

'Good.'

Lana gasped and shuddered in unison as he thrust against her.

'Please stay.' Lana rubbed his shirted back.

'I'm sorry. You know how busy I am at work. I need to be fresh in the morning.' He winked at her. 'And you know if I stay, I won't be fresh in the morning.'

In the taxi, he cursed himself for being lured by Lana and her charms and how she had seduced him with her smile. He shivered and thought how stupid he'd been. A moment of weakness.

He didn't expect things with Lana to take this turn. To cheat on his wife. But then, if that was the case, why the heck was he even seeing another woman behind his wife's back? Still, Owen couldn't stop himself from smiling.

Oh yes, he arrogantly thought. I've still got it.

A few weeks later, Owen surprised Lana when he gave her a small box. 'Is this a …?'

Owen laughed. 'No, it's not an engagement ring. In fact, it's not even a ring for your finger.'

'What?' Puzzled, Lana looked from the box to Owen and back again.

'You know how I like to kiss you from head to toe?' Owen slid his arms around her waist.

Lana nodded, not sure what was coming next.

'Well, I thought it would be nice to see your pretty little toes bedazzled with a fine piece of jewellery.'

Lana opened the box. 'Wow. Is it an emerald?'

'Absolutely.' Owen took the toe ring from the box and held it to the light. 'Amazing isn't it? As soon as I saw it, I thought of you.' He knelt in front of her and began to stroke her legs.

'Owen, that tickles.' Lana stroked her hands through his hair.

'Drop your dress.'

She did as he demanded, and her dress slipped to the floor. She stepped out of it and kicked it away.

'Lovely.' Owen kissed her taught stomach and down to her pink-coloured toes.

He lifted her left foot and slipped the ring on her toe, then stood and lifted Lana into his arms. 'Now let's check it out.'

Lana deliriously smiled and held onto Owen as he headed for the bedroom.

She couldn't be happier as Owen gently laid her on his bed and undressed.

She thought of his bed in his apartment. Lana no longer cared about the sniggers behind her back or the pitying looks from the others in the office.

No matter what, she would make sure Owen Lyle never left her.

Owen was hers, and she was determined to keep it that way.

CHAPTER 7

The deluge of rain made the stone steps into her apartment block slippery. Grabbing onto the handrail, Freya struggled to keep her balance when a thud and gasp behind her caught her attention.

She turned to see the neighbour who lived above her apartment on the third floor, a split plastic bag in her hand, cans of baked beans, a bag of potatoes, and a pint of milk sprawled on the pavement.

'Mrs Harris, let me help you.' Carefully, Freya returned down the stone steps, and took the split shopping bag from Mrs Harris, and stuffed it into her coat pocket. 'Here, I have a spare bag,' Freya said, picking up the shopping. 'I'll carry your shopping, Mrs Harris. You get yourself up those ridiculously slippery steps.'

Mrs Harris smiled at her and clasped her arm around the handrail to steady herself as she hauled herself up the stone steps, eager to get out of the rain.

Inside the vestibule, the heat coming from the radiators hit them.

'Thank you so much, my dear. I thought I'd lost the lot,' said Mrs Harris. 'I've complained and complained to the manager about those steps outside. Treacherous they are. At 78, I need to get about safely.'

Freya pressed for the elevator and waited as it clunked to the ground floor.

'You're the only person I really know in this building, Freya. You know I will miss you terribly. Who will I have a good gossip with?'

Freya smiled. 'I guess you'll have to befriend number 10, opposite you. He seems a nice man.'

'My dear, Mr Winstanley? He must be 90 if a day!'

Freya chuckled and looked at the older woman, who stared up at her with twinkling curious eyes. 'I'm going to miss you too, Mrs Harris, especially your brownies.'

The elevator pinged, and the doors opened. Freya let Mrs Harris go into the elevator first. Once the doors closed, Mrs Harris said, 'Are you getting excited about your move to the countryside? Buying a house without seeing it is an adventure, don't you think?'

Freya sighed. 'I don't know how to feel about it. It wasn't my idea.'

'Hmm.' Mrs Harris checked out the floor-level buttons. 'This elevator takes longer and longer. One of these days, my dear, someone will get in it, and then, whoosh, down the shaft they'll go at 50 miles an hour.'

With a slight jerk, the elevator stopped at the third floor, and the doors slowly opened. Mrs Harris got out, followed by Freya, carrying her shopping.

'Would you like to come in and have tea with me, dear?'

Freya handed Mrs Harris her shopping and smiled. 'I really would love to, but I still have loads of packing to do for the move in a few days.'

Mrs Harris placed a hand on Freya's arm, and gently squeezed it 'Do you have to leave, Freya? If it wasn't your idea and you don't want to leave, then I'm sure Owen will change his mind when he sees how unhappy you are.' Mrs Harris cocked her head. 'You are unhappy about leaving?'

Freya felt her throat tighten. 'Yes, I am. I'm worried it's going to be a big mistake. This has happened so quickly. I always thought Owen loved our apartment, but he already signed all the documents, and the money has gone through, so we're committed.'

'And without consulting you.'

'I'm afraid the apartment was his when we met. So technically, he could do what he pleased with it.' Freya shrugged.

'That is not what a marriage is all about—doing things behind each other's backs, keeping secrets.' Mrs Harris patted Freya's arm, then opened her front door. 'I'm here for you, dear. If you need a chat, any time.'

Freya hugged her and pecked her on the cheek.

'You take care. And I...we would love to have you stay once we're settled in.'

Instead of taking the lift down one floor, Freya took the stairs and waved at Mrs Harris as she disappeared.

'Fat chance,' Mrs Harris muttered.

CHAPTER 8

Owen's hand shook as he unlocked the front door to his apartment. He hesitated for a few seconds and wondered what mood Freya would be in. He stared at the dark blue door as his neck throbbed in tandem with his heart.

Freya's emotional state at the minute was off the scale with everything she'd gone through. And he wasn't helping either, with his mind elsewhere.

Taking a deep breath, he gently pushed the front door open, then closed it quietly behind him. He listened for any signs Freya was home.

Nothing.

No cooking smells came from the kitchen, which was unusual, as Freya loved to cook and always had dinner on the table for him when he came home from work.

'Freya, are you home?'

Silence hit him.

'Freya.' He raised his voice, but it just echoed around the empty apartment. He dropped his briefcase by the front door, slid off his jacket, and hung it on the coat rack.

Gingerly, Owen headed for the lounge.

The room was empty.

Sometimes, Freya would sit by the bay window that overlooked the park across from the main road and people watch, notebook in hand, waiting for inspiration, waiting for the drawings in her head to come through her hands and onto paper.

'Where are you?' He wasn't used to coming home to an empty place.

Owen switched on the two lamps and closed the curtains against the darkening sky.

He looked at his watch. Five pm.

In the kitchen, he switched on the overhead light. A used mug was in the sink. Picking it up, he smelt the inside—it smelled of wine.

Opening the fridge, he sighed at the half-empty bottle of wine. 'Sod it.' he poured himself a large glass and went back to the lounge.

He took a gulp of wine and placed it on the coffee table, kicked off his shoes, put his feet up on the table, and rested his head against the sofa. A heaviness came over him, a tiredness he'd never felt before. He battled to keep his eyes open, but it was a battle he was losing.

'Where have you been?' the woman jokingly pointed a finger at Owen.

He grabbed her around the waist and whispered, 'I'm sorry. Thinking about seeing you got me all excited, so I had to relieve myself while in the shower.'

'Owen! You naughty boy.' She snuggled into him, her hands sliding down his stomach and stopping between his legs. She playfully squeezed. 'I think that's my job, don't you?'

Owen took her head and guided her lips to his.

'Are you dreaming of me?' A familiar voice broke through.

Startled, Owen almost knocked over his glass of wine.

29

'Freya!'

'You were moaning.'

'Where have you been?'

'I didn't fancy cooking, so I picked up some Chinese.' Owen followed her into the kitchen.

'Are you okay?'

'Why wouldn't I be? Hang this up for me, would you?' He took her coat and hung it over his jacket in the hallway.

Returning to the kitchen, he said, 'You normally don't eat takeout during the week. Even at weekends, you still prefer to cook.'

'Well…I fancied a change.'

He wanted to ask her why she fancied a change of food, but her stony face and stiff back, a sign of agitation, suggested to him to keep quiet.

'Tuck in.'

After a few mouthfuls, Owen couldn't keep quiet any longer. 'Come on, Freya, what's the matter?'

'Why should anything be the matter?'

'Don't, Freya.'

She sighed. 'I helped Mrs Harris with her shopping today. Her bag had split, and I had a spare, so I carried it to her apartment.'

'That was very neighbourly of you.'

Freya glared at him. 'She said how much she was going to miss me… us and wished we weren't leaving.'

'She's never liked me.' he reached out for a serving spoon and helped himself to the Chinese food.

With her right hand, Freya reached for the other serving spoon. Owen abruptly grabbed her wrist.

'What the hell's this?' he said, looking at her scratched knuckles. 'How did this happen?'

Freya pulled her hand away and looked at it. 'It looks worse than it is. Leaving the Chinese takeaway, I didn't open the door wide enough, so it hit me as I held onto the door frame to get out. Scrapped my knuckle.' With a quick flick of her hand, she showed Owen again. 'Nothing to worry about.'

'Maybe having half a bottle of wine didn't help.'
He saw her bristle at his comment.

Freya refused to respond to him and helped herself to Chinese.

Owen stared at her. He'd never seen his wife eat like this. Well, eat so much!

'What is going on, Freya? This is not like you at all.' He nervously laughed. Suddenly, he stopped mid-spoonful of food. 'Are you?'

Freya took a bite of prawn toast and chewed it while staring at her husband. The hope in his eyes hit her hard. 'No. I'm not pregnant.'

Owen took hold of her hand. 'Soon, maybe?'

Freya's face turned red and he noticed her clenched fists.

Owen sensed a fuse about to blow.

Suddenly, the Chinese takeaway was up in the air, and the table was on its side; Freya, tears building in her eyes, 'You're a piece of shit, Owen. How could you do this to me?' her words, so softly spoken, Owen wasn't sure what she had said.

But the slap across his face stunned him, 'What the…' he rubbed his stinging face, and before she could hit him again, he grabbed her arms.

'Let go of me.'

'Tell me what's going on?'

'I said let go of me!' she pulled her arms free and ran to the bathroom, slamming and locking the door.

Owen stared at the meal up the wall and over the floor. The corner of the table had dented a cupboard.

Calmly, he set the table right and cleaned up the mess of food.

He could hear the shower running and hoped she was calming down and getting herself together. Owen couldn't handle a loss of control on anyone.

He leaned against the wall, and his hand shook as he pulled out a brown envelope from the back pocket of his trousers and pulled out a photo.

Staring at the photo, he frowned at the couple in the picture on the beach, with the sun shining. The woman in the photo smiled adoringly at the man. Him. While the shower was still running, he quickly stuffed the photo in his briefcase in the hallway.

'You're a piece of shit!' Freya's words went around in his head. Had his wife found out about his…? He couldn't bring himself to say it.

How could he have been so conceited that his wife would never find out?

Of course she has, he thought. Why else would she buy a takeaway, stuff herself silly, and then practically try to tear his eyes out?

The shower stopped running. Hesitantly at first, he gently knocked on the bathroom door.

'Freya, talk to me, please. What have I done to upset you?' He sounded more confident than he felt.

A soft, hurt voice came from the other side of the door. 'Just go away, Owen. I need time to think.'

'Freya, you're scaring me. Please come out and talk.' He paced up and down the hallway, and after a few minutes, he heard the click of the bathroom door unlocking, and then Freya appeared in her bathrobe.

'I don't want to leave.' Her eyes were red and puffy.

Owen took her in his arms. 'I'm so sorry, Freya. Look, it's going to be great. A fresh start.' he searched her face. 'I promise. And who knows, a change of scenery may help.' He patted her stomach.

Freya shrugged and half smiled at the sincerity in his voice.

'That's better.' he grinned. 'You get dressed, and I'll go to the shop and get us another bottle of wine.'

'Or two.' She winked at him.

As he took the stairs to the ground floor, he thought the impending move had affected Freya more than he expected. Was he stupid? Was he arrogant? Selfish even? This move was all his idea. It served his purpose, making his life easier. When buying the house, Freya had been the furthest from his mind.

33

Outside the apartment, as he looked up at the dark sky for some answer, a movement caught his eye. He smiled and waved at the person looking down at him from her third-floor apartment. 'Busy body.' He muttered as Mrs Harris closed her curtains.

As far as he was concerned, the sooner the moving day arrived, the better. He couldn't wait to leave the confines of the apartment block, which had become too small.

Too small for him to hide.

It had been weeks since he had felt claustrophobic, hemmed in every time he entered the building. Even inside his apartment, he felt like screaming at the enclosing walls. And a certain nosey neighbour in the apartment above him, he knew, was keeping tabs on him.

He'd made one stupid mistake. If he was honest, this mess he'd got himself into and Mrs Nosey was the main reason he desperately needed to leave, to put miles between him and the city.

Before he met Freya, it was a fantastic bachelor pad. A week wouldn't pass without Mrs Harris knocking on his front door to tell him, not ask him, to turn the noise down.

Freya changed all that, and she and Mrs Harris, for some unknown reason Owen couldn't fathom, had become friends.

He was convinced the old bat had seen him bring his indiscretion to the apartment. Mrs Harris had said nothing to him, and he knew not to Freya either.

Because if she had, he would be walking around a eunuch by now.

He took the phone out of his pocket. All he needed was only one number, and he typed a message and pressed send.

Unexpectedly, he felt excitement run through him as he imagined the look on the recipient's face when reading the message.

Freya waited for Owen to leave the apartment building before taking his briefcase and sitting in the lounge with it on her lap.

'God knows what I'm looking for?' she looked at Arthur, who lay at her feet. She bent down and stroked him, then sat for a few minutes staring at the briefcase before she opened it and peeked inside. Papers.

She pulled them all out and spread them on the sofa. Most of them looked like advertising sketches and notes. She realised what she was looking for. 'Arthur, I hope it's in here. Something about the house sale. Maybe it can be halted.'

Arthur yawned and stared at her.

Engrossed in what she was doing, Freya was startled when her phone rang. 'Owen, what's up?'

'Nothing, just wondered if you wanted me to pick up some more Chinese?'

'That'll be great.'

'Good, because I've got some. See you in two ticks.'

Panicked, Freya jumped up, and papers fluttered to the floor. Quickly, she stuffed the papers back into the briefcase, really shoving them in, as something at the bottom of Owen's briefcase was in the way. She felt for the obstruction and pulled it out. It was a brown envelope. Freya was about to open it when she

35

heard a key in the lock. She shoved the papers back into the briefcase.

The door was gently kicked open just as she put the briefcase back by the coat stand.

Freya pulled the door open for him and saw his hands full of Chinese takeaway and wine.

'Good timing. Here, take some of this food.' He shoved a couple of bags at Freya and followed her into the kitchen.

'What's up?'

Freya turned to him. 'What do you mean?'

Owen laughed. 'You looked a little flushed when I came in, that's all.'

'Nothing's up, I'm fine.' She smiled.

As he hung his coat up in the hallway, he noticed the briefcase was not where he'd left it. It was now on the other side of the coat stand.

CHAPTER 9

On the coffee table lay a diary, the cover a sparkly pink. Abigail stared at it for a few minutes. She took a deep breath and opened the diary in the middle, where the bookmark was placed.

Four months into my new relationship and I couldn't be happier. But I miss him so much. He's been away, his mum's sick. I hope I meet her soon and she likes me. I like her already.

I wonder if I should send her a get-well card. Damn, I don't know her address. I could phone him to ask for it. No. He'll be mad at me. Gave me strict instructions NOT to call him. His mum might be asleep. I don't want to make him cross. I'll have to wait for him to come back.

Abigail stared at her friend's neat handwriting. 'Why are you so secretive, Lana?' she thought back to the last time she spent a girly evening with her.

'Come on, Lana. Tell me the man's name who's stolen your heart.' Abigail teased her best friend on this rare night with her since she had started dating the mystery boyfriend.

'No! I promised him I wouldn't tell anyone about us, let alone his name. I shouldn't even be telling you I'm seeing him.'

'But you have told me about this budding romance.' She poured more wine into their glasses. 'Don't stop now. Tell me more. I want all the gory details.' Abigail laughed.

'Whoa, getting me drunk will not make me say his name.'

They snuggled into each other. Lana put her head on Abigail's shoulder. 'He is kind and generous, you know?'

Abigail raised her eyebrows. 'Does he have a past? like…marriage?'

'He was once, but his wife died in a car accident.'

Abigail was glad Lana couldn't see her eyes roll. 'Any kids?'

'No. But who knows? I have a feeling about him. He loves me, and…..'

Abigail made a being-sick sound and laughed. 'Yeah, yeah, he's kind, he's generous, blah, blah.'

Lana looked sheepishly at her. 'What?'

'He's, well, he's a bit older than me.'

'No, come on, Lana. How much older?'

'Umm, well, he's forty-five.'

Abigail almost spat out her wine, sat up straight, and stared at her best friend.

'Are you serious? He's 20 years older than you, Lana! Yuck.
He'll be sixty when you're only forty. How gross!'

Lana laughed, 'Hey, don't knock it until you've tried it.
There's no fumbling around, trying to get my bra off, or trying to be cool and not having a clue how to satisfy a woman. He knows how to satisfy me…right down to the last orgasm.'

'You ally cat, you!' They both laughed.

Abigail flicked through the rest of the diary. The last entry was nearly four weeks ago. She returned to the beginning, hoping to see a name or clue.

And there it was.

Owen said he loved me. And I love him. He said we would be together. I will be his wife and live in his fantastic apartment.

A few pages further, Abigail was astonished.

I can't believe what has happened. Owen said he wants me to go with him to look at a house. A house! OMG, is this it? Is he going to ask me to marry him?

Little Lana Young, the girl most likely not to succeed, would marry Owen Lyle, one of the best advertising execs in the city.

Astonished at how much her best friend had kept from her,
Abigail couldn't take it all in. The question that crossed her mind was, why? Lana would always tell her everything, and she to Lana.

It must be this boyfriend, she thought. But who was he?

What secrets was he hiding when he didn't even want to meet Lana's friends?

CHAPTER 10

Spud closed his bedroom door and made sure he locked it. It had got to the point where he had to buy a lock to stop Eric from barging in like he sometimes did, especially when he was drunk, which was becoming increasingly frequent. He was turning into his brother, Spud's father. How long would it be before Eric, too, died?

For a split second, Spud thought, hopefully, soon. He shook the thought from his mind. Even though Eric was his uncle, he had no love for him. In fact, Spud tolerated him. Only because Spud suspected Eric was keeping a secret.

Keeping secrets and lying were the two things his mum had taught him to try not to do because they were terrible traits to have.

Eric had those terrible traits.

Spud was adamant those traits had something to do with why his mum had left.

Since the night she left, Spud had become a serious, sad boy, then an angry, fretful adult.

Eric had told him to lighten up, chill, and get on with life many times. But how could he when all he could think about was his mum and why when he was only ten, she had left him behind?

A mum who he dreamed about. A mum who had left him alone with a father who punched him and left him to fend for himself, sometimes for days, while out with Eric doing who knows what.

From his bedroom window, Spud would sometimes see his mum standing at the bottom of the garden path at the front of the house, but when he ran down the stairs and flung open the front door, she was nowhere to be seen. Where had she gone? Didn't she want to see him, to give him the hugs Spud so desperately missed?

Or was his dad right when he told Spud his mum never loved him?

As the years passed, Spud saw his mum less and less. It hurt him to think she no longer wanted to see him.

From his bedroom window, Spud could see the wood surrounding the house called Blyneath and part of the track leading to it.

He never went there.

The woods held a fear for him. At night, he thought he could hear them whispering to him.

Whispering for help.

CHAPTER 11

The side mirrors shook as Owen tried to navigate the car over the dried dirt track.

'Do you think the removal truck is too close to us?' Freya said as she looked behind her.

Owen glanced in the rearview mirror. 'No. They're fine.'

Freya gazed out the side window as the countryside whizzed past. She felt a heaviness in her heart that he never even considered her in the house move. They were married and supposed to be a team, but he'd totally disregarded her feelings, which hurt her more than she let on.

This was the last place she wanted to live, in an old house that needed a lot of work. And she knew Owen would place it all on her shoulders.

He was good at that. That's what made him successful as an advertising executive. Everyone liked his ideas, and he was good at delegating. And the ladies loved his sense of style.

Too much, she often thought at work gatherings.

As soon as possible, she would hire someone to help with the renovations and repairs. She closed her eyes and breathed deeply. The freshness in the air the further from the city they went, the smell of decaying foliage, the dankness of rotten undergrowth from the woods as they passed, the taste of her life wasting away—and she didn't like it. Trees blurred past, removing her further away from the city she loved, and her heart ached. Ached for the life she could have had, if only.

The journey to their new home had mostly been in silence. With all her being, Freya tried to think of the positives of moving to a house in the middle of nowhere.

But none came.

'You're quiet, Freya,' said Owen, scowling at the road ahead.

'You know why I'm quiet.'

He put his hand on her knee and patted it. 'Come on, I promise you'll love our new home.'

Freya shoved his hand away. Turning from her husband, she wiped a tear away and blinked to stop an entire waterfall of tears from escaping.

Once she knew tears wouldn't flow, she glanced at her husband. She didn't know what to feel anymore. How could he disregard her feelings so totally and not include her in his plans? Did he think that little of her to haul her all the way out here? What was he escaping from? Or, Freya reluctantly thought, who?

Owen kept his eyes on the road ahead. Freya was sure he could feel her looking at him. The veins on his neck were twitching.

'How much further?' she said.

'Only about half an hour. We'll pass through Hartnell village shortly, and then you'll have a chance to take in how quaint this part of the world is and how peaceful it's going to be.'

She looked out her side window again and wondered how he knew how quaint the village was. That was the most he'd talked to her on the car journey to a house she'd never seen.

Feeling worn out, she closed her eyes. Her mind went back to when Owen told her about the house.

'Come on, Freya. It was a bargain. No one else was interested—only me. It's the perfect place to raise a family.'

Owen had shoved the estate agent's blurb about a house needing modernisation with great potential in her hands. 'And it has two acres of land, including woods and a river.'

'If it has potential and in two acres, then why did nobody else go for it?' she threw the leaflet onto the floor.

Owen took her hand and kissed it. 'I know you love this apartment, but it's not good for us anymore. It has many bad memories, for me, at least. Can you understand that?'

She pulled her hand from his and looked out of the bay window towards the park. There, children ran around, played on swings, and kicked footballs. It would have been perfect for their child to grow up and make friends.

'This apartment has been our home for the past three years, Owen. The nursery is ready and waiting for our baby to grow into it.

But you've decided you can't live here anymore. I've been the one who has gone through miscarriages. Had the hope of being a mum taken away from me time and again.' She felt his arms around her waist, his lips kissing her neck.

Owen turned her to face him. 'I know, but all these failed pregnancies have affected me, too. All I want is to start afresh, somewhere where people don't know our past and aren't going to look pityingly at us for not being able to fill a pram. I'm trying to put the past behind us. Make a new start. At least meet me halfway with this one.' He picked up the estate agent's leaflet from the floor. 'I promise you, this will be our forever home. And who knows, maybe a change of scenery and air will help nature along, if you know what I mean.' Much to Freya's annoyance, he patted her stomach.

She turned her back on him and felt physically sick. She knew exactly why he wanted to move as far from here as possible. Mrs Harris.

'Please.' He said, holding out the leaflet to her again. 'Please, for me. Anyway, Arthur will love all the space to run around in. At least let's give it a year, and then if you still don't like it, I promise we'll move back to the city.'

Freya gazed at Arthur, asleep on the sofa.

And so here they were. The removal truck followed behind them as they drove closer to her new home.

Blyneath House.

Dark clouds seemed to hang over the direction they headed in.

Ahead, the dirt track narrowed, and a wide rotten wooden gate, half open and lopsided, blocked their path.

Owen brought the car to a smooth stop. The squeak of the removal truck's brakes behind them echoed in the quiet of the surrounding woods.

As he got out of the car, Owen waved to the removal men to join him, and he waited impatiently as they jumped down from the truck cab. With feet firmly on the ground, the driver yanked his trousers up over his potbelly.

'Well, we're here. Apparently, this is the start of the property.' Owen said, hands on hips and with a wide grin. 'The house is just beyond those trees.' He pointed in front of him.

Past the wooden gate, the woods seemed to swallow the track up.

'Don't know if the truck will get through the gate. It looks narrow and overgrown on the other side.' The truck driver joined him. 'Tell you what… sorry, I've forgotten your name.'

'Eric, and the lackey here is my nephew, Spud.' Eric nodded towards a nervous-looking, thin, red-haired young man.

Owen raised an eyebrow at Eric's description of his nephew; no love lost there, he thought. 'Okay. I'll walk to the end of the track and see how the land lies.'

'I'll join you. That way, I can make a better judgment.' Eric said.

Owen looked at him uncertainly. 'Okay.'

Still in the car, Freya stared after Owen and Eric as they walked toward the gate and squeezed themselves through. Although Eric had more trouble than Owen, which brought a tired, weary smile to her face. She rested her head against the headrest, closed her eyes, and began to curl and uncurl her fingers. It always helped her calm down.

A knock on her window startled her, and she let out a yelp.

'Mrs Lyle,'

She stared at the young man bent over, staring at her. His red hair spilled over his eyes, and as he stood straight, he flicked it away.

'Mrs Lyle, can I talk to you, please?'

The last thing she wanted was to talk to some stranger, but her legs felt stiff, and she needed to stretch them. Before getting out of the car, she checked the back seat. Arthur was sat up, his tongue loped to one side. As Freya opened the car door, the young man grabbed the handle, pulled the door wider, and then moved aside so she could get out. Arthur shot out of the car, headed towards a spot a few feet away, and did his business. After the warmth of the car, the sudden drop in temperature outside made her shiver, and she wrapped her arms around herself against the chill.

'Mrs Lyle, do you think the truck will get through?' he said.

Freya stared at him for a moment. The casual question he had just asked didn't fit with the serious look on his face. 'I don't know, never been here before. I don't know how thick the woods are or how far they go. Do you?'

'I've never been out this way before. No need, really. I've heard the house is in a bad state, derelict, almost.'

'Derelict? What do you mean? I thought it just needed a bit of modernisation.'

'Might do. Like I said, I don't come out this way. Do you want to see where they've gone? To check for yourself if you're concerned?'

Freya's eyebrows raised as she noticed the young man's intense stare toward where Owen and Eric had gone. He seemed to scour ahead, his lips tight.

47

'My husband bought the house, sight unseen, so neither of us knows how the land lies ahead.'

'You mean, you've not been here before, seen the house at all?'

'No, like I've already said.' Freya subconsciously stepped away from the boy when she saw his eyes widen in disbelief. He stared at her, not blinking.

'Why is that a problem?' she asked.

The young man turned his attention back to the woods when voices hit them, and the two men came into view.

They waited in silence for Owen and Eric to get to them. Owen waved at her and shouted something, but she couldn't understand what he was saying, so she just shrugged.

At her side, Owen said, 'It's okay. There's enough room for the truck to get through the trees, then the track opens up into a big wide driveway leading up to the house.'

'Which, Mrs Lyle, looks very impressive. Very impressive indeed,' Eric said. 'It needs work, though. But I reckon it'll be worth it. Great foundations, from what I can see. Come on, Spud, let's get going. It's getting late, and I want to get back to civilisation before it gets dark.'

Sulkily, Spud followed his uncle back into the truck cab.

Freya called to Arthur as Owen got back into the car. Once settled on the back seat, and Freya in the front passenger seat, they slowly made their way up to the house. The removal truck trundled behind them. ,

The track up to the house wasn't much of a track. Made up of loose stones and fallen branches, with moss and weeds growing everywhere.

Finally, Freya was relieved to see first-hand the house that had caused many arguments between her and Owen.

When she saw the house, she wanted to cry and head straight back to the city.

There was something about it that was completely wrong.

Freya got out of the car and shivered as ice-cold air seemed to surround her. She gasped at the intensity of the feeling and looked around her in despair.

Weeds grew through the gravel, and dandelions peeped through the cracks in the paving stones.

The paint on the front door had peeled, leaving an ugly, damp mark. Window frames were rotten, and some window panes had cracks running through them.

Freya glared at Owen, open-mouthed. 'What the hell have you done?' It took all her strength not to go at him and slap the smug look on his face away.

'Freya, it's great.'

She stepped toward him. 'Great? Are you bloody blind?' With a shaking hand, she pointed at the house. 'Look at it.'

Owen did just that, then shrugged. 'Yeh, it's a bit overgrown out here, in front, but we can sort that.' He grabbed her wrist and dragged her to the front door. 'Come on, it's better inside.'

'You've been in already?' Freya said exasperated with Owen.

'Just a quick look, didn't we, Eric?'

'Sure.' Eric and Spud leaned against the truck, waiting for instructions and enjoying the domestic squabble before them.

Freya dug her heels into the ground and tugged her hand free.

'I'll follow you,' she said, rubbing her wrist where Owen had grabbed it.

'Please yourself.'

The front door creaked open, and Owen, full of bravado, bounded through the front door.

Reluctantly, Freya followed, but at the front door, she suddenly stopped and grabbed hold of the door frame. A musty, damp odour hit her, and she had to put a hand over her mouth to stop from gagging.

'So, what do you think?' Owen stood in the middle of the hallway. Light from the open doorway lit up his face.

Behind him, she could see stairs leading to an open landing. She looked over the hallway, dismayed at the mould on the walls, and dust particles danced in the disturbed, thick, dank air. To her right, double wooden doors were ajar.

Freya looked left and saw a sliver of light under a door.

'That's the kitchen.' Owen said.

'Kitchen?'

'I'd say so because I peeked through the window, and there it was.' Owen darted to the kitchen door and pushed it open with a 'Tada!'

Freya's heart sank as she peered into the kitchen. She felt Owen's hand on her back as if to push her in, but she shrugged him off.

An old wood stove was against the far wall, surrounded by dusty worktops with suspicious dropping here and there.

A couple of cupboards hung off broken hinges.

The worst for Freya was the black-and-white lino floor, ripped in places and thick with dirt and dust. Her feet stuck to some unknown mess. She grimaced. 'Has someone been in here already? Look at these footprints.'

Owen looked over her shoulder at the spot she was pointing at in front of the stove. Two fresh-looking footsteps were marked in the dust.

'They don't look like footsteps to me, just smudges.'

Above the badly rusted steel sink, a double window looked out onto the woods across the driveway, where Eric and Spud stood by their truck.

Owen took her hand, led her back across the hallway toward the double wooden doors, and shoved them open with his spare hand.

'Look at the size of this lounge. It's twice the size of ours.'

The lounge had a log fire on the outside wall, with a bay window that looked out onto the front garden to the same view as the kitchen. The other window overlooked the back garden.

'Back gardens more overgrown than the front.' Freya couldn't hide her disdain for the place. She shuffled her feet, and dust swirled around them.

'Do you realise we'll need help with the garden and the house?' Freya said, deflated, as she stared out into the overgrown back garden.

She heard his footsteps coming up behind her, and then Owen's arms encircled her waist. Freya closed her eyes against his uninvited touch.

'Don't you worry about that? What I saved on this place will more than cover any hired help.' Owen squeezed her. 'So, what

do you think about this place now? I know your softening, thinking about help.'

Without waiting for a reply and without warning, he slapped her behind and headed out of the room. 'Come on, there's unpacking to do.'

Freya hated him.

Spud stood at the front door carrying a box with 'Kitchen' written in big black letters.

'Don't just stand there, the kitchens that way,' Owen pointed.

'I'm just going to put the box down here.' Spud put the box down in the hall and slid the box to the side of the door.

'What are you playing at?' Owen scowled at Spud.

Spud checked behind him to see where Eric was. He was headed toward the house, a lamp in his hand.

'I'm not going inside' Spud shook his head.

'I've paid you to empty our apartment and to put our belongings in their designated rooms here. You've done half a job, now finish it.' Owen stood in front of Spud, who continued to check behind him.

'No, I won't. This place is bad.'

'Is there a problem?' Eric said as he got closer and noticed the anger on Owen's face.

'He,' Owen pointed at Spud, 'Is refusing to do the job he's being paid for.'

Eric put the lamp down on the gravel. 'What's the matter now, Spud, eh?'

'I don't like this place. It gives me the creeps. It's a bad place,
I can feel it.'

Owen bellowed, 'If you don't do what we've paid you to do, there'll be no bonus.'

'I don't care.' Spud ran back to the truck and, once inside, locked himself in.

Eric sighed and shook his head. 'He can feel things, so he tells me. I think he's just work-shy.' he picked up the lamp and passed Freya and Owen. 'I'm afraid you'll both have to help. Forget the bonus. I'll talk to the boy.'

'Great start.' Freya headed to the removal truck. As she passed the cab, she looked up at Spud, who, after a few seconds, quickly turned away.

A few hours later, Eric climbed into the truck's cab and, without saying a word to Spud, started the engine, stuck his hand out of the open window, and waved at an unhappy Owen and a tired-looking Freya. Neither of them waved back. As the truck bounced away from the house, Eric turned to Spud. 'What the hell do you think you're playing at? We could have had a good bonus out of those two if you'd not been so paranoid about old houses and dark woods.'

Spud hunched up against the truck door, his hands under his armpits. 'I'm not paranoid. It's a feeling.'

'And how many places have you had a feeling about, then, eh, Spud? Tell me because I don't understand you.'

'Only this one.'

Eric laughed. 'Bloody hell, Spud, you dickhead.'

Spud turned to face Eric and put a hand on his arm. 'I felt a bad vibe in that house. Like something.... bad had happened or is going to happen.'

'Make your mind up. What am I going to do with you?' Eric scowled and shook his head. 'And take your fucking hand off me.'

Spud gazed at the side mirror as the truck passed through the rotten wooden gate. Suddenly, a shaky image of a woman standing by the gate startled him. She wore a calf-length dress, and her dark, limp hair hung over her face.

He squeezed his eyes shut and shut, then quickly opened them again.

The woman was gone.

Spud glanced at Eric, who gave no sign he had seen anyone behind them.

CHAPTER 12

After all the furniture and packing boxes had been dumped in the hallway and the truck had left, neither Freya nor Owen was in the mood to sort out which room anything went into.

Freya's head throbbed, and her shoulders and arms ached from carrying. She needed to stretch her legs, and Arthur needed a walk or a quick run around the garden.

She called Arthur, who had been lying by the double lounge doors. He shot up and, avoiding the boxes in the hallway, bounded to Freya.

'First, a run around in the garden for you, Arthur.' Freya opened the front door and watched Arthur bound outside and head to the back of the house. Within seconds, he was back at Freya's feet, panting and wagging his tail.

'Okay, okay, here I've got your favourite ball.' She pulled the red rubber ball out of her coat pocket and threw it ahead of her into the woods.

The ball bounced high several times before landing a couple of feet in the woods. The sound of fallen leaves crunched under the ball's landing force.

Arthur bounded after the ball, and as usual, his tongue lopped out the side of his mouth.

He was going at a full sprint when he suddenly stopped, making him roll over himself.

Inside the woods, he lay down, his ears flat against his head, looked back at Freya, and growled.

'Go on, Arthur, go get your ball, and I'll throw it again.'

Arthur growled again, hunched up, and backtracked out of the woods. Once out, he headed straight for the open door.

'I'm sure he gets sillier every day.' Freya strolled to retrieve Arthur's ball and waded through the calf-high undergrowth. As she bent to pick up the ball, ahead of her, a branch snapped. She peered into the semi-darkness of the wood, its shadows lengthening in the disappearing sunlight. Squinting, she thought she saw someone. Nothing but a swirl of mist that seemed to caress the trees. She shook her head, thinking it might be a rabbit, fox, or other small animal that had made the noise.

Another louder snap sounded, but it came from behind her this time. Twisting, she almost lost her balance. A mist seemed to form around the trees behind her, too. Again, she shook her head, and in the dimming light, she convinced herself she was tired and seeing things,

Freya rubbed the back of her aching neck and hurried out of the woods, not looking back until she reached the house.

Once through the door, she gripped the side and, looking toward the wood, slowly closed the door.

The sense of foreboding came to the fore again, just as it had when she first entered the house, and she didn't like it. The trees swayed in the breeze as if nothing was wrong.

No strange shadows moved silently through the woods, only those made by the trees. All seemed normal, but the churning feeling in the pit of Freya's stomach told her otherwise.

That evening, after they had done all they could with placing boxes and furniture in the right rooms, Freya and Owen, exhausted, relaxed in the lounge.

'I'm telling you, Owen, something's not right. The feeling I had when I came inside the house was the same as I had in the woods.

And when Arthur wouldn't go in after his favourite ball, well, I think there's something in those woods. And I don't like it one bit. It scared the hell out of me.' Even though her hands shook a little, Freya took the glass of wine he offered her.

He sat on the sofa beside her with his glass of wine. 'Look, it's been a hectic day. We're both tired. Moving is stressful at the best of times, and this is all new to you.'

Freya sipped her wine. 'Moving's stressful, all right, especially if you didn't want to move in the first place.' Freya avoided looking at Owen's hurt face.

'How many times will you throw this move in my face?' He placed his glass on the small side table.

Freya handed him her glass of wine, then headed for the stairs. 'I'll throw it in your face as many times as I like. Oh, by the way, there was a strange, disturbing smell in the woods.'

As she crossed the hallway, she heard Owen sarcastically mutter. 'Woods smell, Freya. Animals, rotten vegetation. Heck knows what's died in there.'

Owen picked up his wine and stared out the lounge window and gulped down his and Freya's wine.

He wondered if there was anything else in there.

Hiding. Waiting for him to slip up.

No, he pushed the thought away.

He knew he had made sure his secret would stay hidden.

CHAPTER 13

Her hand moved the branches aside from her face. She wanted to see clearly who the woman with the dog was.

Despite the trees' protection, when a stick snapped under her foot, she was certain she had been spotted. The sound seemed to reverberate around her.

The woman with the dog looked up.

At first, Lana thought she'd been seen, but another noise behind the woman distracted her.

A soft hand touched Lana's shoulder. They watched as the woman with the dog hurried back inside the house.

The swirl of mist around them made them both grateful the woman hadn't seen them.

But what if she had?

Lana had stared straight into the woman's startled eyes. She must have seen her.

'No.' Rose whispered. 'She didn't see you. She couldn't see you.'

'Why?' Lana said, her voice so soft, so low.

'Because you, we, don't want her to see us. Yet.'

Lana nodded. 'But who is she?'

CHAPTER 14

Spud had always avoided Blyneath House and the surrounding woods.

When Eric told him about the removal job they'd got, he was horrified at the prospect of going anywhere near the woods and the house.

'No, Eric, don't make me go up there.'

Eric had turned on him. 'I'm sick and tired of your whining. We're doing this job. End of. Understand? And in case you don't quite get it, we need the money.'

What choice did Spud have?

When they pulled up outside Lyle's apartment block in the city, Eric went into the building, leaving Spud to open the back of the truck, ready for furniture and boxes.

While waiting for the job to start, Spud took in the surrounding area. It looked peaceful enough. Across the road there was a park with a play area. It didn't seem built up like some cities Spud had seen on television. The area had a friendly look to it. It was hard for Spud to understand why anyone who lived in a nice place would up and leave for an ominous place like Blyneath House.

He glanced up at the apartment block. A woman stared out of the window towards the park. Her face was the saddest he'd ever seen.

He waved when she glanced down at him, and the woman half-heartedly waved back.

Owen Lyle was a different story. He was bouncing off the walls with excitement at the move to the country.

'Hay, come on, I'm paying good money for you slow coaches to move my stuff.'

'Don't worry, Mr Lyle, we've got it all in hand. Anyway, what's your rush? We've got all day.' Eric said as he handed Spud a box with the word kitchen in black ink.

'Because I can't wait to start a new life with my gorgeous wife, that's why.'

'Yeah, your wife.'

Owen glared at Eric. 'Something to say?'
Eric said nothing.

'Good.'

Spud hated Owen Lyle on site. But what baffled Spud was that, out of the corner of his eye, he saw Owen Lyle quickly lean into Eric with a scowl.

'Don't push it,' he heard him say.

And now he had Eric on his back, telling him he was paranoid. If anyone was paranoid, it was Eric. Spud had heard the nightmares he had. The screaming of his mum's name.

He wondered how the hell Owen Lyle knew about Eric, who he was, where he lived, and what he did to earn a few pounds if, as Freya had mentioned, neither she nor Owen had ever been to this area before.

Eric had moved in after Spud's mum had left, supposedly to help his father look after him. Eric had a grand view of how Seth had treated Spud, ridiculing him even from a young age.

'Your mum was nothing but a whore. You stop this shit telling me she comes here. She's gone. Gone with some low life from the pub. You'll never see her again.' His father would taunt him.

Spud would burst into tears, and his father would just laugh,

'She ain't coming back for you. Never.'

As Spud grew older, he often thought about those words: 'gone with some low life from the pub'.

When his mum left when he was ten, he couldn't grasp what his father was telling him. But the truth is he saw her run out of the house from his father's temper, and his father ran after her, grabbed her and dragged her away from the house.

He had waited hours, looking out his bedroom window for his parents to return.

Only his father returned. Wet from the rain and his trousers covered in mud. Had his dad shouted at him? Spud couldn't remember or didn't want to remember.

His mum had told him his father could be a bitter man. She'd had enough of him and would have left him years ago, taking Spud with her. But she had nowhere to go and no money.

The fact only his father had returned that night had always played on his mind.

The first time he saw his mum after she had left was on his way back from school. As soon as he saw her, his heart raced, and he thought his mum had come back home. Come back for him.

61

She stood at the bottom of their garden path, arms wide, waiting for him to run to her.

Spud had dropped his school bag and ran to her, the sun in his eyes making him squint. He ran and ran but didn't seem to get any closer.

Gasping, he had to stop and bend over, holding his knees to catch his breath.

He looked up to find her gone. He stood there for a few minutes, thinking, where did she go?

Spud ran back to his house and, once inside, shouted, 'Dad, Dad, I've seen her, Dad, I've seen mum.'

He ran into the living room to find his dad sprawled on the sofa, the television showing horseracing.

Spud shoved him, trying to wake him up. 'Dad, dad, wake up.'

Seth groaned and grouched awake. The can of beer in his hand bounced on the floor and frothy beer poured out onto the carpet.

'What the hell is wrong with you, boy?' Seth sat up and shoved Spud away from him. 'Get me another beer.' He slurred at his son.

Spud, on the floor, stared at his dad. His greasy grey hair stuck to his head, and his unshaven face was coarse. The stain of a runny egg he'd had for breakfast that morning was encrusted in his beard.

'Dad, I've seen Mum. She's back, she's here.' In his eagerness to tell his dad of his mum's return, Spud didn't notice his dad's fist come around and punch him in the side of his head.

'Don't you mention that whore in this house again, understand? Ever. You hear me, boy?' Seth yelled.

Spud nodded. Tears pricked his eyes, and as quickly as his shaking legs could take him, he ran out of the room.

Eric stood in the kitchen doorway, twisting a tea towel in his hands and a sad look.

Spud glared at Eric. 'I hate him.' Spud sobbed, and he ran up the bare stairs. The stair carpet his mum had bought just a few months ago had been ripped up by Seth and thrown into the back garden, along with all the other rubbish his dad wanted to get rid of.

In the far corner of the garden, behind the overgrown vegetable patch his mum had lovingly attended, was a dusty black bin bag full of his mum's clothes. Discarded.

On his bed, Spud had cried, not because of the pain in his shoulder where his dad had shoved him with his foot or the punch to the side of his head, but because he knew he'd seen his mum.

He felt her warmth radiating from her and the smell of her perfume, even from a distance, a flowery rose scent. His mum's favourite.

When his uncle Eric moved in with Spud and his dad, Spud felt so alone. Eric and his dad always seemed deep in conversation, and whenever he entered the room, they would shut up. But the look on his dad's face, the haunted look in his eyes, and his palled skin told a young Spud those conversations were not good ones.

But then, Spud's dad had died. The drink finally got the better of him. Eric had stayed around, but he was a broken man, and that's when his nightmares reverberated around the house in the early hours of the morning.

Now, twenty years on, Spud stared out of his bedroom window for a different reason.

CHAPTER 15

After her disturbance with Arthur in the woods yesterday and Owen's total dismissal of her feelings, Freya seriously despised Owen. They hadn't spoken at all that morning, and Owen went to work without a kiss or an 'I love you.'

Freya was fine with that. The more she stayed in this damn house, the more her resentment toward Owen grew. In her mind, she wouldn't stay much longer in the house or with Owen.

If he didn't leave with her.

The morning autumn sun still chilled Freya as she and Arthur walked to the village to get a few supplies. She felt desperate for fresh air and wanted to give Arthur a long walk.

Breathing in the crisp, clean country air gave her some energy, and Arthur waddled happily beside her.

Freya passed through the rotten, lopsided gate at the bottom of the track from her house, and she made a mental note to have the gate fixed as soon as possible.

She thought about her first night in the house and how it had been a fretful one. She had tossed and turned, and a face, a blurred face, infiltrated her dreams.

And a whisper filled her head.

She couldn't make out exactly all the words, but she could make out one of them.

Help.

It disturbed her, but she put it down to the stress and tiredness of moving.

Following the slow-flowing river to her left, Freya smiled as Arthur, now filled with confidence, dipped his nose and paw into the water, scuttling back at its coldness.

In the distance, she could see a bridge.

Owen had pointed out the village of Hartnell as they drove through it yesterday. Freya wasn't the slightest bit interested in her husband's opinion that it looked quaint, whatever he meant by that.

Until they came to the first bridge after the village, over the river.

According to the sign next to the bridge, it could not support the weight of the removal truck, so their car was touch and go. They had to return to the village and take another road.

Owen ranted about why the removal men hadn't told him about the bridge, and even Freya was astonished the removal men had mentioned nothing about the bridge. As Owen had told her, the removal men were from around Hartnell.

Crossing the bridge, she followed the river through fields of dying meadow flowers.

Ahead, she could see the spire of the village church. 'Every village should have one.' She said to herself.

Arthur, in front of her, sniffed out his new surroundings and looked to be enjoying the freedom to roam somewhere other than a park.

He bounded in and out of the woods to the left of the small meadow. 'Don't go too far, Arthur, I don't want you to get lost.' Her voice echoed around her. Barking, Arthur came running out of the woods. His tongue flapped out to one side, as it usually did when he was happy, and his tail eagerly wagged. He bounded ahead of her.

Freya could feel the sun on her face and wished she'd put on a thinner coat. She smiled as Arthur darted across the track into the woods.

She thought it was strange, watching how happy he was out here in this part of the woods, but back at the house, something spooked him.

And her.

Freya walked the rest of the way to the village in glorious satisfaction that, at least, this part of the move was worth it. The trees looked spectacular in their autumnal colours, unlike those Arthur refused to go into, which looked lacklustre with their leaves already on the forest floor.

Soon, the village church clock appeared splendent with the sun on its dial.

Freya walked down from the track and over another small bridge, as the river had now turned to her right in front of her. She put Arthur back on his lead.

'Wow,' Freya gasped as she entered the village centre. Small shops surrounded the cobbled square, and a memorial monument with flowers was in its centre. 'Come on, Arthur, let's look around.'

Looking from left to right, Freya took in the brightly displayed windows of the shops.

A wool shop had balls of wool in all the rainbow colours in the window. There was a nick-knack shop, a tearoom, and, to her delight, a small bookstore. And a place Owen would like: a quaint-looking village pub.

She soon spotted a small convenience store. 'We'll go there last, Arthur. Don't want to be carrying shopping around.' She headed for the bookstore, eager to look in the display window.

Freya was so engrossed in the books in the window that she didn't notice someone come up behind her.

'Do you like to read?'

The voice behind her surprised her and made Arthur bark. She turned to see a young man with dark curly hair and deep green eyes smiling at her. Involuntarily, she felt her heart rate increase.

'I'm sorry if I made you jump.' The man bent down and stroked Arthur.

'That's okay.' Freya breathed out. 'I am an avid reader, and there is a good choice from the looks of it.' she pointed at the window.

'I'm Nathan. I live just outside the village.' He pointed in the opposite direction she had come in. 'How are you finding the house?'

'The house?' Freya couldn't help but be drawn into his fresh face.

'Blyneath House? I'm right in thinking you're the new owner. There's not much the village doesn't know about the goings on.' He brushed his hand through his dark hair.

'Oh, yes,' Freya stuttered and hated herself for it.

'It's been empty for a long time. I bet it needs a lot of work done on it.'

'You're not wrong there. It looks like I'll be the one doing all the organising and getting someone in to do the jobs I can't do.' Arthur lay down between them both and shut his eyes.

'It is a big house.' Nathan bent and stroked a contented-looking Arthur again. 'I could help with the overgrown gardens, do a bit of DIY, and maybe update electrics if you'd like some help.'

Freya wondered. 'Have you been to the house?'

Nathan smiled. 'Not in a while.'

Freya nodded. 'Then that would be great.' Freya watched as Arthur let Nathan stroke him again. 'Do you know about the house? I mean, about its history?' she said.

'Well, the previous owners didn't stay long. I suspect it was too much for them.'

'Oh. Why was that? Weren't you around to offer your services?' Freya smiled.

Nathan looked around at the small number of people mingling around, who gave a sly look at the two of them. 'I guess they didn't come into the village to find out.'

Freya followed his gaze and nodded, then looked down at a contended Arthur dozing on the pavement.

'My husband, Owen, just doesn't have time to do anything, which is ironic, really, seeing as it was his idea to buy the house. I had no idea what he was up to until he came home and blurted out he'd bought a run-down house and signed all the papers in his name only because he wanted to surprise me. He was so excited, and I was gobsmacked.'

'Do I sense irritation?'

Freya felt her cheeks burn. 'I'm sorry. I didn't mean to say that.'

Nathan pulled a card from his jacket pocket and handed it to Freya. 'Talk it over with your husband and call me if you want my help.'

'I'll be in touch, definitely.'

Nathan bent to give Arthur a last tickle. 'My name's Freya Lyle, by the way.' she said as he passed her.

He turned to her. 'I know.' he smiled and crossed the square.

Nathan glanced over his shoulder back at Freya. She was staring back into the bookstore window, and Arthur, now wide awake and tongue lobbing out of his mouth, watched him, or so it seemed.

He turned left down a side street, paused and leaned against the white-washed walls of a house.

Breathing deeply, he peeked around the corner to take in one more look at Freya. She was walking away from the bookstore toward the convenience store.

Nathan took to her straight away. He felt kindness and loyalty from her, which shocked him, as he didn't even know her.

The feelings he felt were mixed, good but also of dread.

It frightened him.

Why?

He couldn't work it out.

CHAPTER 16

'So, you decided to employ a complete stranger to work on OUR home?'

Owen paced up and down in the lounge, walking across the inherited threadbare, red-patterned rug that Freya had repeatedly tried to get the dust out of.

'What do you want me to do, Owen? I can't do everything on my own. I need help.' She watched as he downed another whiskey. She hated it when he drank. He was an obnoxious drunk. 'And you said to get help, seeing as you're back in the office and have no time to put effort into restoring this house *you* bought.'

'I told you I'd do all I could.'

Freya took the glass of whiskey off him and placed it on the small side table next to the sofa she'd been sitting on. 'How can you when you're not here?' she accused him, then looked out of the front window. 'It was you who bought this house without consulting me. And you begrudge me wanting to hire someone to help with the outside, inside and in between.'

Owen came to her, put his arms around her waist, and kissed her neck. Feeling her stiffen from his touch, he let go.

'I can't help it if work keeps me away from here. It's my job that'll pay for all the renovations.'

'Your job kept you away from our apartment, too.' She turned to face her husband and felt a touch of guilt for her harsh words.

Owen tried to keep the hurt of her words from his face. Did she know? He thought.

Freya stared at him, opened her mouth to say something, then decided against it.

'What do you want to say to me, Freya? Come on, spit it out, don't hold it in.'

Freya said quietly. 'I know more than you think. And I'm going to bed.'

Owen laughed at her. 'I think you need to chill. I know this move has been stressful for both of us.'

'Don't patronise me, Owen.' And before she slammed the door behind her, she turned to him. 'You railroaded me into this house.

I think the least you could do is let me sort it out how I see fit.'

Owen flung his arms in the air. 'You're right. I'm sorry. I'll make it up to you, I promise.'

'Don't leave it too long. You never know what's around the corner.'

Before he could ask her what she meant by the remark, she was out of the room. He picked up the whiskey and drained the glass.

A shudder went through him as a coolness overtook the room, and he suddenly felt a deep urgency to check out the woods.

CHAPTER 17

On the second night in the house, Freya's dreams again were disturbed by a blurred face she couldn't make out. She turned one way and then another, waking to face the back of her deep-sleeping husband. She wondered what he was dreaming about.

A sudden bang from outside the bedroom door startled her. Instinctively, she pulled the covers up to her chin and glanced sideways at Owen. Still asleep. Slowly, she lifted the bedcovers and swung her legs out of bed. The cold floor under her feet made her shiver.

Warily, she made her way to the bedroom door. Leaning in, she placed her right ear against the door to hear what could be outside her bedroom.

She pulled the door handle down and, bit by bit, opened the door.

Before stepping onto the moonlit landing, she looked back at Owen, then clicked the door behind her.

'What the hell are you doing?' she muttered as she tip-toed down the landing.

To her right was the handrail. She looked down onto the hallway below. To her left was the wall along the landing. Further down the landing, an empty room was directly opposite her bedroom.

To the right of the empty room was another bedroom over the lounge, where Owen had insisted they put the spare bed. It was smaller than the empty room and a tight squeeze, but he was adamant that was how he wanted it.

The empty room at the end of the hallway was to remain empty until he decided what to do with it.

When they first moved in, the room was empty of any usage. Freya had wondered if it had been a nursery, office, or playroom. She didn't want an argument with Owen, so she said nothing and let him have his way with the room.

Freya made her way along the landing. Her hand skimmed along the old, faded, and ripped wallpaper.

She found the switch for the small table lamp they had placed under the window and clicked it on.

Nothing.

She flicked it up, then down again.

Still nothing.

Both she and Owen never thought to check if it worked. They had just placed it there and plugged it in.

'Nathan. I'll put it on the list for him.'

Leaving the comfort of the wall, she grabbed the handrail and peered over.

'Arthur.' she whispered. 'Arthur, have you got out of the kitchen again?'

The moonlight seemed to dance through the window, casting shadows down the stairs. Then she heard it: a rasp behind her and a hotness-like breath on the back of her neck. She whirled around. Feeling her head spin, she grabbed the handrail before losing her balance.

Blood pounded in her ears, and she suddenly felt sick. She took a deep breath when another sound caught her attention.

'What the…' The sound was the creak of a slowly opening door, coming from the direction of the empty room at the end of the landing.

Unnerved, she tried the lamp again. This time, a faint glow emitted from the small bulb. Cautiously, Freya looked down the landing toward the door.

It was ajar.

She glanced from her closed bedroom door to the open one, unsure if she should wake Owen. But curiosity got the better of her, as she knew the door had been closed when she'd gone to bed. It was always closed. Owen had insisted.

Step by slow step, she made her way down the landing.

Suddenly, she stiffened, and all her senses screamed at her to stop, not take another step towards the empty room, and return to her safe bed, where her husband was sleeping.

A voice in her head, the one in her dreams.

Help.

'Hello. Who's there?' she whispered as she slowly made her way down the landing again.

The room that Owen said could be left to the last, the one he said he didn't feel comfortable in, but he couldn't answer her when she asked why.

She shuddered.

And when a hand clasped her shoulder, she screamed.

'Freya, what the hell?'

A voice she recognised broke through her foggy brain, and she opened her eyes to see Owen leaning over her.

Freya grabbed hold of him. 'Owen, I thought I heard something.'

'Thank god.' He stroked her hair. 'Are you okay? What the hell were you dreaming of to make you scream so bloody loud?' 'What?' she realised she was in her bed, covered. 'I... I wasn't dreaming,' Freya blinked. 'I felt...I felt someone behind me, their breath...'

'Freya, you were sitting up in bed screaming, 'Let go of me, let go of me' scared the shit out of me.'

'But I'm sure...'

'It's still early in the morning, and I've got a big day ahead.
And you need to plan for the hired help. Try to get back to sleep.'

Owen kissed Freya on her forehead, turned his back to her, and was soon snoring gently.

Owen's rejection of her experience upset her so much that she couldn't sleep. She gazed up at the ceiling. What the hell was going on? She knew she hadn't been dreaming; it was too vivid. Abruptly, she pulled the covers off her and stared at her feet.

Dirty.

Something wasn't right. And deep down, she knew, no felt, it had to do with this house.

After a few hours of restless sleep, Freya finally decided to get out of bed. She must have slept some, as Owen's side of the bed was empty, and she hadn't heard him get up. She pulled on her jeans and jumper and put her hair in a ponytail.

The sun's rays through the landing window looked like fingers stretching down the staircase. They mesmerised her, and she couldn't move.

Freya couldn't help it. Her eyes flickered towards the room at the far end of the landing, the one that was ajar last night but now, in the sun's light, was closed. Before she realised, she was moving toward the door, her eyes fixed on the door handle. Her feet moved like they had a mind of their own.

Standing in front of the closed door, she hesitated. The chill in the air caught her breath, and her hand trembled as it hovered over the door handle.

'Freya, what are you doing?'

The sharp tone made her spin around, and she found Owen at the top of the stairs glaring at her. 'I asked you what you were doing?' he said, stepping towards her.

'Nothing. I don't know.' She wiped her sweaty hands on her jumper as she walked to him.

'I thought we'd agreed to leave that room till last.'

His grip on her shoulder hurt, and she pushed his hand off.
'Cool it, Owen. I know you don't like that room, for whatever reason, but there's no need to have a go at me because it doesn't bother me.'

Owen held his hands up. 'I'm sorry.' He headed downstairs to the kitchen and shouted back to Freya. 'A quick coffee and I'm off.
I'm late as it is.'

Freya entered the kitchen as Owen gulped down the last of his coffee.

'How are you after your bad dream last night?' he rinsed out his cup.

Freya hesitated, not ready for another argument to start the day. 'Fine. I guess moving to a new house, an old, spooky house at that, with all its strange noises, could bring on some subconscious dream,' she said, hoping the answer would satisfy him.

'That's good. What plans have you got for today? Is the handyman coming?'

Before she could answer, he passed her and headed for the front door. Freya followed him.

'I think so. While I'm waiting for Nathan—that's the handyman's name, by the way, I'm going to look around the house more. There are nooks and crannies around here I've not checked out, and I might have a walk through the woods to see if I can find what's making Arthur avoid the front.'

Owen opened the front door, letting the chill of the autumn morning blow inside.

'You mean you're going to look into the room at the end of the hall? Even though I've specifically said not to, we've already done that, haven't we?'

Freya took a deep breath. 'Yes, a quick look. But we haven't really looked in the other rooms, I mean down the cellar.'

'Be careful, okay? Anyway, I've already been down the cellar, and it's full of junk from the previous owners, no doubt.'

She followed him out to the car. 'You never mentioned that to me,' she said, folding her arms.

'Like I said, it's just full of junk. No reason to go down and have a look now, surely.' He threw his jacket on the back seat. 'Maybe later in the week we can both go down to the cellar and look through the junk. Might find something useful, who knows.'

Freya waved until the car disappeared from view.

'I'll look where I want, you prick.' Arthur sat patiently beside her on the driveway. 'Go.' Freya laughed as Arthur bounded to the back of the house.

Not the front, she thought.

Freya stared at the part of the woods that spooked Arthur. From where she stood, they looked like any other wood, dark and mysterious, if you let them.

She shivered and was glad when Arthur came bounding back and headed inside the house.

Before she closed the front door, Freya watched as a mist headed toward the house and swirled through the trees.

She headed to the kitchen where an eager Arthur was waiting for his breakfast, and if she had looked out of the kitchen window, she would have seen someone watching her.

CHAPTER 18

Spud didn't want to talk about anything. All he wanted to do was sleep and dream about nothing.

Since Owen and Freya Lyle had moved into the house a few days ago, his dreams of his mum had begun again after years of not seeing her in his dreams. The dreams were blurred, but he knew it was her. He could never forget her smile.

His lack of sleep made him angry at Eric, who wouldn't let up about how much bonus Spud had lost them because of his 'silly' nonsense about feeling things. And he kept saying Spud had to go and see the Lyles to apologise, and on hand and knees if need be.

Not a chance.

He had felt lost since his mum had left and was convinced his father had made her leave. He wasn't sure about the part Eric had played yet, but he would find out. It had been too long. He had taken too long to really find out why she had left.

His whole soul seemed to have left him in a state of sorrow. And since his father passed away, things had got worse. Eric had become more insufferable, a pain in his backside.

'Don't be so stupid, boy.' Eric had yelled at him when Spud was a young boy and had told him about the dreams of his mum he was still having.

'If you were dreaming of your mum, why in hell not your dad?'

Spud knew the answer to that but didn't want to tell Eric how he hated his dad in life and death and how his gut feeling told him he'd done something to his mum.

The funny thing was, as soon as he found his father dead on the kitchen floor, the first person, well, the only person he had called, was Eric. And now Eric walked around as if he owned the place. Eric made Spud feel like he was the lodger in his own home.

When Spud became old enough to take care of himself and inherit the house as he should have, Eric kept fobbing him off, telling him the feelings Spud kept having and the strange sensation that something terrible had happened and would happen, no court in the land would give him his so-called birthright. From then on, Spud vowed never to mention his dreams to Eric again.

Unless.

Mrs Lyle seemed nice, and he didn't want whatever was happening in the house to hurt her.

As for her husband? He was nasty. He sensed it the moment they met.

'Be careful, don't drop the glass box, don't scrape the sideboard on the door side.' All that morning, Mr Lyle barked order after order at them while they tried to empty his city apartment as fast as they could.

Eric took it in good grace, eager to finish at the other end and get a good bonus.

That had always struck Spud as odd. Mr Lyle was excited about the move, but his wife just sat on the window seat with her dog, watching as they loaded the truck. She hardly said a word.

'Spud, are you coming down for breakfast?' Eric broke into his thoughts.

He opened his bedroom door and leaned over the handrail. 'Yes.'

At the small kitchen table, Spud pulled out a chair and sat with a flump. The cooked breakfast looked good, and as he tucked in, he realised how hungry he was.

'So, you going to see the Lyle's about apologising for your rudeness?'

With a mouthful of beans, Spud said. 'I told you I don't like the place.' He took a slurp of tea.

'Spud, we need the money. Go on, be a good nephew and apologise. You might be in luck. Mr Lyle might not be there.'

'Oh, why?'

'When I picked up some supplies in the village yesterday, I overheard a conversation in the butchers that Nathan Smith, you know the handyman, yeah, handy at what is how I see it.' Eric winked. Spud rolled his eyes. 'Anyway, he was spotted talking to Mrs Lyle in the village square and he gave her his business card.' Eric snorted at this.

'So, to me, that means Mr Lyle isn't there to do what the house needs.' 'Mrs Lyle seems sad.' Spud stared into the cup in his hands.

'What?' Eric stuffed another piece of bacon into his mouth.

'Nothing. I'll go around in a day or two. Let them settle in first and make sure Mr Lyle won't be at the house.'

CHAPTER 19

Abigail sat opposite the police officer, her fingers tapping on the desk as she waited for him to finish reading the part in the book she'd given him to read.

'Well, what do you think?' she was becoming impatient. 'Officer, what do you think?'

He looked at her over his thin-rimmed glasses, closed the book, and placed it on the desk. 'It's a pretty interesting read. You found the book on Lana's bedside table?'

Abigail nodded, 'Yes, we each have a key for the other's apartment, you know, in case something happens or we lose our own key.'

The Officer placed his thin bony hands under his chin and sucked on his mint. 'How long have you known Lana?'

'Since high school. Look, Officer, Lana has been missing for four weeks now. This isn't right; something is wrong. I've not been able to get in touch with her – at all.' She paused and was close to tears. 'But I keep getting texts from her. I don't understand why she would do that. We'd talk at least once a day, you know, hear each other's voice.'

'I can understand your concern, really, I can. But there are procedures to follow.'

He tapped the closed book with a bony finger. 'This is very interesting. I'll have to show my superior, but I'm not sure what else we can do. Lana is a grown woman; if she wants to go away for a few weeks, that's her choice.'

Abigail dabbed at her eyes and then pushed back her chair.

Although she didn't want to, she shook the officer's hand when he offered it.

As she headed for the door, he asked. 'Tell me, Abigail, have you ever met this boyfriend of Lana's?'

'No, like I've already said, I knew she was seeing someone, but she said it was all hush-hush for now. Her boyfriend apparently wanted her to himself before she introduced him to anyone.'

Abigail waited for the officer to say something else. 'What was his name again?'

At the door, she sighed at the officer's constant doublechecking. 'Owen. That's all I've got.' She left the room but poked her head back in. 'Lana said he was 45 years old and lived in an apartment uptown. He has a fancy job, so she said. It's all in the diary.' 'I see.' The Officer nodded.

Abigail hesitated at the open door. 'Do you think he's got something to do with her disappearance?'

The officer shrugged, being very non-committal, which annoyed Abigail.

Seeing the exasperated look on Abigail's face, he relented.

'Don't you think it's strange the woman he was seeing has disappeared, and he's not trying to contact any of her friends?' he said.

'That thought has crossed my mind. But if Lana's boyfriend hasn't met any of her friends, how would he know where to find us?

And the only conclusion I have is that he didn't know us. Maybe Lana hadn't mentioned us to him...yet. Maybe she only told me Owen didn't want to meet any of her friends to keep me quiet.'

The officer came around his desk, sat on the edge, crossed his arms, and gazed at her.

'Could he be hiding something?'

'Like what?'

'Perhaps he's married?'

Abigail thought about what Lana had said. Her boyfriend was a widower, but she thought better than telling the officer that. She didn't know why, but her gut was telling her to keep that information to herself, for the time being, at least.

It was becoming complicated. She would have to check out this Owen herself.

CHAPTER 20

Freya checked her watch again. It was 9.30 am. Nathan had told her he'd be at Blyneath at 10.00 am. Even so, Freya couldn't wait to see him, and now the mist had dispersed, she kept looking out the lounge window.

She heard the van before she saw it and rushed to open the front door, stepping aside to let Arthur run out of the house to do his thing at the back.

In his small white van, Nathan came into view and stopped in front of the house, in front of Freya.

Seeing him made her smile.

Nathan opened the driver's door and seemed, to Freya, to glide out of the van. He waved to her, even though she was just a few feet away, the smile on his face as big as Freya's.

'Good morning, Nathan. I'm glad you could make it.' Freya greeted him as he opened the back doors of his truck.

'Morning, Freya, and I'm a man of my word.'

She noticed how tidy and in order the inside of his van was. Tools were in boxes on the right side, and other odds and sods were in little wooden boxes on shelves.

'What would you like me to do first?' he asked, looking over at the front of the house. 'It looks like you have some rotten window frames. They'll need fixing first, I reckon; otherwise, the wind and cold will whistle through the house.'

Freya followed where his finger pointed to the lounge window. At the top right-hand corner of the wooden window frame, she could see a hole the size of a fist.

'Well, that explains why the room gets so cold.'

Nathan hauled a black box from his van, placed it on the ground, and closed the van's back doors.

Freya followed him as he walked along the front of the house and pointed out a broken pane of glass in the kitchen window.

'I've not noticed that before, ' Freya said, looking closer. It must have happened recently. It's strange.'

'Not to worry. I'll put in a piece of wood to replace the glass for now. The hole in the window frame and cracked glass in the top right window will need to be repaired first, and then I'll fix the hole in the lounge window frame. Have you any ladders?'

'Follow me.'

Freya led him to the back of the house and down an overgrown, short path. 'Luckily, the previous owners left some tools and ladders in the outhouse.'

Nathan tugged at the wooden outhouse door. 'It's stiff.' Finally, the door flung open, and Nathan peered inside. 'Wow. What a find. Fancy the last owners leaving all this gear. It must have cost a fortune. Some could do with a cleanup, but that won't take long.'

Freya looked over his shoulder. 'Yep, some people. Why would anyone leave all this stuff?'

Nathan shrugged. 'Maybe they didn't have the room where they moved to, or maybe not even a garden.'

'Well, use what you need to, Nathan. I'll put the kettle on. In my humble opinion, you can't start work without a good brew first.'

'Thanks.' He could smell her fresh floral perfume when she looked over his shoulder. He liked it.

Nathan eyed Freya as she made her way back along the overgrown path. But a movement at a top-floor window in the middle of the house caught his eye.

It was such a fleeting movement that he wasn't sure. He knew it wasn't Owen in the house as Freya had rung him earlier to check if he was still coming to work on the house and had told him Owen had already left for the city hours ago.

Anyway, it wasn't any of his business who else was in the house.

'Teas ready.' Freya appeared with a tray, two mugs, and a plate of biscuits.

Taking a mug off the tray, Nathan said, 'After boarding up the broken pane, I'll mow this grass. It'll be easier to get to the outhouse.'

'Great.' Freya put the tray down on the ground.

They stood there for a few minutes, drinking tea and looking around them.

'Nice cup of tea,' Nathan finally broke the silence.

'Thanks.'

Nathan handed Freya his empty cup. Their fingers touched, and a fleeting pause between them had her looking up into his deep green eyes, which stared into hers.

She felt a hotness on her cheeks and a feeling she'd not had in a long while. Her pulse raced.

At that moment, time seemed to stand still, leaving only the desire and a promise, a far-away possibility of a promise.

She could sense the intensity radiating from Nathan as his fingers stroked hers.

A bark from behind broke the spell between them as Arthur came bounding toward them.

CHAPTER 21

Lying on top of the bedcovers, Spud couldn't get the thought of Mrs

Lyle alone in that house out of his head. He didn't know why he felt this way. He just did.

Since the removal day, when she walked past the truck after he refused to enter the house and looked up at him, he was sure he'd seen her mouth 'help', but he looked away quickly, so he might have missed what she said if she'd said anything at all.

A loud bang from the kitchen directly below his bedroom broke through his thoughts.

Spud sighed and opened his bedroom door and peered over the landing. Even though it was midafternoon, he could see the kitchen light was on.

'Eric, is that you?' Spud called as he descended the creaky, bare stairs.

Whenever he went up or down the stairs, the cold under his feet always reminded him of the day his mum had bought the stair carpet they once had, ad hoc, a roll end, and wanted to surprise his father.

She had been so happy to tell Spud how little it had cost, and his dad would be relieved. Spud had looked at the carpet, not interested. What ten-year-old boy would be?

As usual, his father had come home late with a few beers inside him, and he'd hit the roof at his mum spending money on the house without his say-so.

In fact, his father was always mad at his mum for spending money on anything other than food and beer.

'What the hell were you thinking of? Are you stupid?' He'd heard his father shout at his mum as he listened from the top step.

Spud had noticed this from a young age: his father rarely used his mum's name, Rose.

'Seth, it was cheap. We need a stair carpet. Going up and down the stairs in cold weather and getting splinters. I thought enough was enough.'

A sound of a slap, then a gasp. Nothing new in that, Spud had thought.

'Seth, it was a bargain. I thought you'd be proud of me.'

'I don't care how much it didn't cost. You know how strapped for cash we are.'

'If you didn't join your so-called mates down the pub every night, we'd have more than enough money for lots of nice things.'

'Get out of my sight.' his father had yelled, as his mum ran up the carpeted stairs.

Spud jumped up from the top step and hurried back to his bedroom before she caught him earwigging on their arguments—again.

His parents' bedroom door slammed.

He could hear his father in the kitchen throwing stuff around in his drunken state. Spud knew the mess would be there for his mum to clean up in the morning. And she would.

Spud gently pushed open the kitchen door to find Eric sitting at the table, his head in his hands.

'Eric?' Spud sat opposite his uncle. 'Eric, have you been crying? What the hell is going on?' Eric never cried, Spud thought, not even when Seth had died.

Eric looked up at his nephew. 'I'm okay, Spud, honestly. I've got something on my mind, that's all.' He looked at Spud and thought how much he looked like his mum.

'What have you got on your mind that'll make you cry?'

'It's nothing, really.' Eric wiped at his face with his shirt sleeve. He was wearing the same clothes he had on yesterday.

'Doesn't look like nothing, Eric. You're really upset.'

Eric sighed and pushed the paper that was in front of him towards Spud, who looked down at the headline.

'Just went to pick up the paper and saw this. Young woman missing for four weeks.'

Confused, Spud looked at his uncle. 'That's sad, but why would this news upset you? Do you know her?' he tapped at the picture of a young blonde-haired woman. Eric shrugged. 'I guess I'm just getting sentimental in my old age. But she was so young.'

'Was?'

'I mean, she's been missing for four weeks. Doesn't look good, does it?'

They both stared at the picture in silence for a few seconds.

'I guess. Anyway, you're not that soft. Eric. I know why you're upset.'

Eric looked sharply at Spud.

'It's the 20th anniversary of my mum's disappearance.'

Eric shuffled, shoulders slumped, to the kitchen window and leaned on the kitchen sink. He looked out into the back garden and sighed. If only Spud knew, he thought. Spud had just made it easy for him to change the subject.

'Stupid, I know, but your mum was like a sister to me.'

Spud shook his head. Sometimes, Eric would go on about his mum, especially after he'd been drinking, and sometimes it would be embarrassing. Spud reckoned Eric had been secretly in love with her.

He had to change the subject.

'What do you think happened to her?'

Without turning around, Eric murmured, 'Your mum…I don't… know.'

'No, Eric, I mean the missing girl in the newspaper.' Spud stared at Eric's back

'It's anyone's guess, but it's so sad. So young.'

The old wooden chair scratched on the tiled kitchen floor as Spud joined Eric at the window. He was a few inches taller than Eric, although when looking at them side by side, Spud seemed taller by more than that. The stoop Eric had didn't help.

Spud peered out of the kitchen window into the eeriness of the mist of the sun's rays. 'I bet her family are frantic, not knowing where she is. I can understand that because I've had enough of not knowing.' Spud reflectively said.

Eric glanced up at his nephew, his set jaw, and the steeliness in his eyes. Then he put a hand on Spud's shoulder.

'I need to stop thinking about mum and why she left and start doing something about it.' He looked down at Eric. 'Since I was ten,

Eric, for the last twenty years, I've done nothing, nothing but think.' Spud headed for the kitchen door but stopped at the table and tapped on the picture of the missing girl. 'This has reared my frustrations and anger about where my mum is.'

'Has this to do with your nightmares? And the strange feeling you keep getting? Especially at Blyneath? When we lost a bonus because of your feelings, I don't understand you, Spud. Cos I'm sure you can go see someone for that problem.'

Spud sighed at his uncle's insistence, even when he thought he was being helpful, that his feelings of dread and evil, yes evil, were all in his head.

'I think you should go and lie down, Eric, then get a shower. You look like shit.'

Spud closed the kitchen door behind him.

Eric glanced at the newspaper again, at the young blond-haired woman who was missing.

He wiped his eyes and sat back down at the kitchen table. Eric had wondered time and time again how he had got himself into such a mess.

What he witnessed four weeks ago at Blyneath House distressed him.

And it disturbed him that Owen Lyle was an easy liar.

CHAPTER 22

It was only the second day for Nathan at Blyneath, but he felt uneasy as he pulled up outside. He wiped his sweaty palms on his jeans. Yesterday, he had seen something that made him uncomfortable, not when he was out in the back garden when he thought he had seen someone in an upstairs window. No, this was different. He squeezed his eyes shut to recall the image he had seen while fixing the hole in the top, far right window frame.

While busy sanding the outside of the frame, he suddenly felt uneasy, like he was being watched. Hesitantly, he glanced into the empty room.

There stood a young woman staring at him.

Startled, Nathan almost fell off the ladder but managed to grab the windowsill and steady himself. He took a deep breath and looked back into the room.

It was empty.

The house gave him the creeps, and he thought he was beginning to imagine things

'Hello, Nathan,' Freya's voice cut through his thoughts. He'd seen the paper this morning before coming to Blyneath, and the resemblance between the woman he thought he saw in the empty room and the picture of the woman on the front page of the newspaper disturbed him. He decided not to say anything to Freya about what he had seen yesterday.

When he saw Freya's smile, a calmness overcame him.

'Hi.' Nathan got out of his van and accepted the mug of tea Freya held out to him.

'Thanks.'

'So, what are your plans for today? By the way, you did a good job on the window frames yesterday. You can hardly tell where the hole had been.'

Nathan nodded, then took a sip of the tea. 'I think I'll start on the overgrown grass at the back of the house today.' He nodded in that direction. 'I said I would do it yesterday, but the frames took longer than I expected and I thought they were more important.'

'That'll be perfect. I want to build a studio there so I can paint.'

Nathan followed Freya to the back of the house, and as soon as he could, he glanced up at the top back window. Nothing.

'You're a painter? Is that why you moved here, for the peace, quiet, and inspiration.?' He stopped himself. 'I'm sorry, I just remembered you telling me this move wasn't your idea.'

Freya shrugged. 'I've always painted, off and on, but when I met Owen, the painting took a back seat. Actually, I don't know why; I had the time. Once we were married, Owen wanted me to stop work and look after him.'

Nathan raised an eyebrow.

'I know old fashioned, but I was in love then and wanted to please Owen.'

Nathan couldn't help but pick up on the words *was in love then*. But he decided it was none of his business, so he said nothing.

'I guess moving out here will give me the time to take up my painting again. After the work on the house and the garden has been completed, of course. Even if it's reluctantly on my part, this move could be a blessing in disguise.'

They walked in step until they reached the overgrown section, where they placed their cups on the ground.

Nathan couldn't help it. He put his arm around her and turned her to him.

Freya looked up at his face and was ready for him to kiss her.

Ready and desperately wanting him to kiss her.

'Can I ask you a question, Freya?'

Freya looked at him. 'Of course.' Instinctively, she parted her lips, waiting.

Nathan felt his stomach jump, which took him by surprise.

He couldn't keep his eyes from her full, parted lips, how he wanted to kiss her, to hold her and kiss her, to make love to her. Then he looked into her eyes, her blue, tired eyes.

Nathan stepped back, not trusting himself to go where he shouldn't. 'I just want to know if Mr Lyle is okay with me doing the work on the house. I mean, some men don't like another man doing jobs they could do. Makes them look.' he paused. 'It makes them look unmanly. Does that make sense?'

Freya felt herself blush. 'Call him Owen, Nathan. The Mr title may make him believe he's important here as well as in the city.' She had to calm herself.

Calm her feelings for the man in front of her she hardly knew but wanted to, so passionately, get to know.

Nathan forced a smile and a laugh but felt neither was sincere.

97

'Owen commutes every day?'

'Yep, that's why you're here, Nathan. So, Owen has no argument about you being here, helping. I didn't want to move to this decrepit house. I never even knew my husband had bought it until after the papers were signed. He bought it in his name. How about that for a partnership of marriage?' She shrugged, thinking what Mrs Harris had said to her.

'I would have been really pissed about that.' Nathan realised he sounded harsher than he should have.

Freya, brows crossed. 'He'd already sold our apartment…well, his apartment. I moved in after we were married. It never crossed my mind to ask Owen to add me to the deeds, and Owen never offered.'

Freya shrugged again. 'But it's not so bad here, look?' she twirled, arms outstretched. Unsteady, the twirl brought her close to Nathan, and as her hand brushed against his chest, she felt the rapid rhythm of his heartbeat through the fabric of his t-shirt. Her hand rested on his chest.

Nathan put his hand over hers. His touch ignited a spark within her. He slowly brought her hand up to his lips and gently kissed it. His kiss on her hand sent a sensation through her; she couldn't help it. She gasped.

Freya pulled her hand away as calmly and cheerfully as she could. 'All this space and Arthur loves it. Well, most of it, anyway.'

Right on cue, Arthur came bounding round the corner, ears flapping, tongue out.

Freya knelt and hugged Arthur. 'Hay, Arthur, who let you out of the kitchen?'

Instinctively, Nathan glanced again up at the window. 'I'll get on with clearing this area for you, Freya. It might take me a couple of days. There's so much of it.'

'In answer to your question, Nathan, Owen always leaves, even sometimes before first light, to drive to the city. He's tried to work from home but gets frustrated by the lack of Wi-Fi. But he's never been the DIY type.'

Nathan bent down and tickled Arthur behind the ears. 'That's good. Then I can get on without looking over my shoulder.'

Freya watched Nathan as he made his way to the outhouse. She felt a longing for him she thought stupid. She'd only just met him, and she didn't know him.

But.

CHAPTER 23

Abigail had had enough. She was back at the police station, waiting impatiently to speak to someone again about her missing friend.

Finally, an officer called her to follow him into an interview room. A few minutes later, the same police officer she had first reported her friend missing came into the room and sat in the chair across the table from her.

'Nice to see you again, Miss Hall.' Officer Parnell smiled.

'Like I said last time, Officer Parnell, call me Abigail. And no offence, it's not nice to see you again.'

Officer Parnell smiled but nodded in agreement. 'So, how can I help you?'

Abigail leaned across the table. 'I've been very patient with you. Days ago, I reported my friend Lana was missing, and she's still missing. Nothing seems to be progressing.'

'We are doing all we can, but it's a bit difficult considering she's still in contact with you.'

'But she's not. It's not her, I know it. If Lana wanted to speak to me, she'd actually speak to me, not text, and it's strange I can't contact her. Her number's blocked.'

'I see. But you must see it from our point of view, Abigail. Lana seems to be in touch with you. You've shown us the text messages, so to us, she's not missing; maybe she doesn't want to be found.

Abigail sighed. 'I know it sounds very plausible, Officer, but she's my best friend, and I know her better than anybody else.'

Officer Parnell said. 'You said her apartment looked undisturbed when you found her diary.'

'I know. But it's so strange. Why would she be, the way I see it, hiding from me?'

A knock on the door interrupted the conversation. Officer Parnell opened the door and took two plastic cups of tea from the person on the other side of the door. He placed one of the plastic cups in Abigail's hand.

'Yuck looks like dishwater.'

'I know, and it tastes like it.'

Abigail had to smile.

'Her boyfriend been in touch?'

'Not a word. Why would he if Lana never mentioned me to him.'

'Just you?'

Abigail looked at the tea in the plastic cup and placed it on the table. 'Lana is a very quiet person. I'm her only real friend, and we would always, well, used to, spend all our time together.'

'Until this mysterious boyfriend came on the scene.' Officer Parnell took a sip of his tea and shivered in disgust. 'Maybe said boyfriend has something to hide?'

'You tell me, Officer Parnell, because I haven't got a clue.'

'I know it's hard for you. But our hands are tied at the minute as she's allegedly in contact with you. I'd be worried sick, too. ' He leaned toward Abigail. 'Look, you have a key to Lana's apartment.' Abigail nodded.

'Why don't you stay at her apartment for a few days? Wait for her to turn up,' he suggested.

'I thought about that, but what if she comes back and is angry at me?'

'I'd be angry at Lana for not telling me where the hell she'd been and what had she been doing.' Officer Parnell quipped.

CHAPTER 24

Owen stared, without seeing, down at the traffic and the people below scurrying like little mice as if their lives depended on getting wherever they were going as quickly as possible.

'Did you hear what I just said?'

Startled, Owen turned to face his boss, who stood with his hands in his trouser pockets, shirt sleeves turned up, and a concerned look on his face.

'I'm sorry, Alan, I've got stuff on my mind, and I've not been sleeping.' Owen sat back down at the oval oak table in his office.

'Everything okay at home? How's Freya getting on with renovating the house?'

Owen snorted. 'Like every woman, I guess. She got help. Some local lad. Supposed to be the local go-to handyman, he's been at the house a couple of days now, and I have to say it does look like he knows what he's doing.'

Alan raised his eyebrows. 'Concession indeed, Owen Lyle, the man who never backs down.'

Ignoring his boss and friends' dig at his brutal competitiveness, Owen flicked through the papers on his desk, ready to be signed, but he did not see the words. The words were there but made no sense to him. It was all a blur of black and white.

'Looks good to me, Alan. I think we'll make a good deal with this one.' Owen tried to sound confident.

'My thoughts exactly.' Alan refilled their empty coffee cups. The last thing Owen wanted was more bloody coffee. A stiff whiskey was what he craved right now. They'd only been in the house almost a week, and it was already becoming apparent to Owen that it was a mistake. A big mistake on his part.

Alan sat at the table and spread a newspaper in front of him. 'Poor lass. She's been missing for four weeks now. There's no hide or hair of her.'

Owen leaned in to see who Alan was talking about. He jolted in his seat and knocked his coffee over, which spread across the picture of the woman in the photo. 'I'm so sorry Alan.' He scrambled, took a hanky out of his trouser pocket, and tried to mop up the coffee.

Alan sighed and headed for the office door. 'Don't worry, I'll let you buy another one.' Alan grinned as he closed the door behind him.

Once the door closed, Owen had to put his head between his legs. He felt he was going to pass out. After a few minutes, he lifted his head, and from the corner of his eye, he glanced at the picture of the woman. He didn't want to look at or read about her. It was too close for comfort. Questions were being asked. 'Why did she quit? Where did she go?' were the usual ones. But curiosity got the better of him, and he pulled the paper toward him and read the full report.

'Lana Young, 25, has been missing for four weeks now. She failed to turn up for dinner with a friend, Abigail Hall, who reported Lana missing after many failed attempts to contact her. Stating that Lana had exciting news to tell her, so why would she vanish? Abigail said Lana is a lovely, kind person, and she'd gone through a lot. Friends of Lana, an only child whose parents had passed, are urging anyone who has seen her or knows where Lana is to please call the police.

The paper points out an interesting point: Abigail told police she knew Lana was in a relationship but didn't know her boyfriend.

Lana wouldn't tell her, wanting to keep it a secret for now. Abigail urges, as do the police, for the mystery boyfriend to show up and talk to them.

'Interesting reporting Shana Thompson.' Suddenly, his office door opened, and Alan poked his head in. 'No need to get me a paper,

Owen. I've borrowed your secretaries.' Alan shut the door as quickly as he had opened it.

Owen sat back in his chair, rocking back and forth on its spring, and stared at the ceiling, pondering if he had done the right thing. He wondered if he could have worked things out.

To his advantage, of course.

CHAPTER 25

When he pulled up, Owen was glad Nathan's van wasn't in the driveway. He wasn't in the mood for pleasantries. Although from the work Nathan had already done, he was pleased with the work.

The only thing he knew about the handyman was he was about Freya's age.

Owen was not sure how to take this. Freya was 15 years his junior, and even though he never showed it, he knew the younger in his firm were coming up behind him, ready to take his crown. He was ready for them. But was he ready for a young handyman to be alone with his beautiful wife? His insecurities surfaced again. He would have to meet with the handyman, whether he liked it or not.

The thought of Freya being in the company of a younger man played on his mind. He was well aware of his greying hair and his spreading girth.

Freya had worked as a temp for his Advertising Company— well, it was not actually all his, as he had told her. But he was second in command after the big guy, the boss, and the company's primary engine, Alan.

Freya had been so impressed that she agreed to dinner with Owen.

But he had to confess to her he was second in command. Alan had invited Owen and Freya out for dinner with his wife.

Freya had asked Alan how he would enjoy his retirement without having reached the dizzy heights of CEO over a younger man.

Owen had felt the floor leave from under him.

Thankfully, Alan, his long-time friend, had taken Freya's comment with good grace and had even laughed so loud heads turned in the restaurant to stare.

Owen was grateful to Alan for his light-hearted response to Freya. However, Alan gave him a gentle reprimand in the office the following morning.

Gentle or not, it was still a telling-off, and Owen had felt humiliated.

Even though he and Alan had been friends for many years, there was still a boundary not to cross between Top Dog and Owen.

He never told Freya about his slap down. It was better to keep the status quo with Freya; in her mind, she was dating a very ambitious and soon-to-be CEO man.

Now, it seemed Freya was more at ease in the house and willing to stay for at least a year.

As soon as he opened the front door, a smell hit him. He sniffed and followed where it was coming from.

In the kitchen, Freya, with Arthur lying in his basket watching her, stirred what smelt like Bolognese sauce on the stove.

Owan put his arms around her waist and nuzzled into her neck.

'Stop it.' She giggled. 'You'll make me burn the sauce.'

'Thank you.' He stepped away and topped up the glass of wine on the table.

'For what?' she turned down the heat on the hob and took the glass of wine he held out to her.

Owen bent and kissed her on the cheek. 'For making me my favourite dinner,' he said, laughing when Freya playfully hit him.

Arthur barked, wanting attention, and padded over to Owen, who stroked him from top to tail.

'So, how was your day?' Freya asked, turning back to the sauce and stirring it.

Owen took off his suit jacket and hung it over a chair, undid his tie, folded it and placed it in the centre of the table, sat down, and kicked off his brogue shoes.

'That's better.' He stretched his arms into the air, then back down. He gulped the wine. 'Ready for that.' He sighed. 'Anyway, my day wasn't too bad. The usual shit, just a different day. Alan running around like a headless chicken.' He took another gulp of wine. 'And getting upset by the bad headlines in the papers.' He glanced around the kitchen to check if Freya had bought a paper.

'So, what news has upset him this time? Someone lost a cat or had a bike stolen?'

'Not quite.' He saw the paper on the worktop next to him, reached for it, and glanced at the headline page.

'Have you read the paper yet?' he said.

'No, I've been busy.'

'Apparently, a woman has gone missing. No one's heard from her for weeks.'

'Oh! Now, that would upset me.'

Freya stared at her husband as he read the front-page article. She had skimmed through the paper but took little notice of the article on the front page. Bad news made her sad, and she avoided it as much as possible.

Bringing the bottle of wine, she sat opposite Owen and refilled his glass.

'Who is the missing woman?' she reached for the paper.

'What?' He pulled the paper nearer to him, out of her reach. 'I don't know. A young woman from the city. I think Alan's upset because his daughter, Alice, is the same age as the missing woman.' He shrugged and folded the paper.

'That's sad.' Freya lunged for the paper, unfolded it and read the front-page headline. 'At least she was not from around here, you know, with me spending a lot of time on my own.'

Owen shrugged and folded the paper over to cover the headline. He'd had enough of seeing the blond-haired woman staring out of the paper.

'You look tired', she said. 'The long commute back and forth to your office. It's not good for you.' Heck, she thought, they'd only been here a week, and Owen had aged ten years, it seemed to her.

She stared at him over her glass, at his grey hair and slight belly. The lines on his face had only appeared in the last few months, and his disinterest in her became increasingly apparent. He seemed distracted, like something was on his mind and not just work. Freya felt he was keeping something from her.

Then she thought of Nathan when he had touched her and her wanting to kiss him. Right now, that was the last thing she wanted Owen to do to her.

109

Arthur plonked himself down by Freya's feet and snuggled in.

'I don't think you're alone.' Owen laughed, pointing at Arthur. 'Anyway, you have that handyman, Nathan? He's here all day, isn't he?'

Freya shrugged, 'I guess.' She went back to the stove, stopping to stare out of the kitchen window into the woods. The dark was coming in quickly, encroaching on Owen's dark blue car, making it invisible.

In her mind's eye, she saw Nathan waving goodbye for the day as he got into his white van.

She smiled, but it faded when she saw Owen's reflection in the window. He looked intently at the article about the missing woman, even though he'd just been dismissive of it.

'Nathan's doing a good job, by the way. He's cleared a lot of the overgrown grass at the back.'

'I'm glad.' Owen folded the paper. 'Now you can see how the place could look.'

Owen joined her at the window. 'It's getting dark earlier now,' he said, wrapping his arms around Freya's waist.

She nodded and smiled at the reflection of her and her husband.

Over his wife's shoulder, Owen glanced out into the night. The sway of the trees against the dark sky.

He suddenly shuddered.

'Are you okay?' Freya asked as she felt his shudder

'I'm fine. Just need food and the love of a good woman.'

Freya half smiled and set the kitchen table. Owen looked towards the woods again.

At the darkness.

The darkness that played with him.

The darkness that whispered.

CHAPTER 26

The view from the woods was a good one. The lights in the kitchen lit up the room like a beacon to ships at sea.

She watched with dark, sad eyes as he kissed the woman she thought she had seen a few days ago, but her days were not at all. They were just light and dark.

They seemed to laugh. Laugh at her? Her head ached, even to the touch, and her stomach sagged like a heavy shopping bag. She looked down past her stomach to the dried blood on her legs.

What was happening? She didn't like it in here, in the dark woods. She wanted to be in that house with Owen; him kissing her, not the other woman cooking something on the stove.

Owen liked her cooking. He said it was like she'd been given a gift from above to satisfy him.

She'd laughed at his poetic nonsense, but she loved it, and she loved him.

And he loved her.

He'd always tell her, especially after they'd made love.

She stepped forward, dry fallen branches and leaves crunched under her feet. An urgency was getting the better of her. She desperately wanted to know who the woman was with Owen.

Had Owen told her? She felt she should know, but the pain in her head, in her whole body, wouldn't allow it.

A gentle, calming hand rested on her shoulder, a comfort to her in this dark time. A time she didn't understand.

CHAPTER 27

Freya was still annoyed with Owen, even now, over a week later, about his rush to buy this place without her knowing, without him asking her, his wife. She'd never seen a for-sale sign outside the apartment, but Owen had said someone from his company had bought it.

But one thing always niggled at the back of her mind.

Had Owen been to the house before? Knowing how to get here without using a Sat Nav. When she'd asked him, he just laughed it off, telling her the estate agent gave him good directions, which she found hard to believe.

What about the detour around the village because of the weak bridge? How did he know that?

When she asked him about it, he just shrugged and said Eric had told him. But that was a lie. Owen was angry about the detour, shouting at her as if it was her fault that the removal men hadn't told him about the bridge.

She gazed out of the kitchen window while drying a cup. The wind was becoming stronger, and the branches and trunks of the trees swayed hypnotically.

Suddenly she said. 'Come on, Arthur. It's time for a walk.'

Arthur, always eager for a walk, bounded to her and waited while she put on her boots and coat and put Arthur's lead in her pocket.

Nathan had phoned earlier that morning, saying he needed to go to the city to pick up some supplies and would be back later or tomorrow.

Her heart sank at the news that she might not see him today.

But there was always tomorrow to look forward to. Quickly, she reprimanded herself, telling herself she was a married woman.

Arthur's curiosity about sniffing every leaf, patch of grass and tree trunk along the muddy track held no bounds and made Freya's walk to the village slow and lengthy. But she loved it.

Earbuds in, and in her own little world, Freya could only think about Nathan, to the point she never noticed Arthur ahead of her had stopped and was looking at her.

That's when she felt a hand grab her shoulder.

Freya screamed and spun around to find a young woman standing in front of her.

'What the hell? You scared the shit out of me,' Freya squelched away from her.

'I'm sorry, I didn't mean to scare you, but I called out...you obviously didn't hear me.'

Freya took out her earbuds and put them in her coat pocket.

Arthur waddled up to them and shook the mud off his coat, splattering them both. 'Ugh'. They said together, shielding themselves.

'I'm sorry.' Freya put Arthur on his lead.

They both stared down at a cheeky-faced Arthur, tail wagging and tongue out.

'My name's Abigail. Can we walk and talk?' she looked into Freya's eyes.

Taken aback at the intensity on Abigail's face, 'Why? I don't know you,' she said.

'I know, and I'm really sorry to have to talk to you, but you're my last hope. It's about my missing friend, Lana.' 'Lana? The woman in the paper?' Abigail nodded.

'I'm sorry to hear your friend is missing, but what does it have to do with me?'

Abigail touched Freya's arm. 'It concerns your husband, Owen. That's his name, isn't it?'

Freya felt her heart drop. 'Owen? Owen Lyle?'

Abigail nodded. 'I know something about him, something that's unpleasant.'

Freya stepped away from Abigail, shaking her head. 'What is my husband to you?'

Abigail took a deep breath and shoved her hands in her coat pockets. 'I think he was seeing Lana when she disappeared.'

'What! That's ridiculous. He's married to me. Owen would never have an affair. Never.' Freya was surprised at her own indignation at the thought Owen could have an affair, but her own feelings for another man mocked her.

'I know. I'm sure he does. But that hasn't stopped people from having affairs. Anyway, Lana thought he wasn't married. In fact, he told her he was a widower. I read it in her diary.'

Incensed, Freya tugged at Arthur and made to pass Abigail.
'I see, you snoop at people's private thoughts as well as tell blatant lies about someone you don't know.'

'But I *do* know, and I'm not lying, I promise.'

Freya, brows furrowed, stared into the eyes of the woman standing in front of her. The disturbed, scared eyes. 'Okay, tell me how you know. And how the hell did you find me?' How?

Abigail started with the information in Lana's diary: 'Owen, the top executive at a high-end advertising agency, lives in a swanky apartment uptown.'

First, she acquired the names of the top agencies in the city and then went to their web pages to see who was who in the company.

It didn't take Abigail more than two hours to find the person she was searching for. Yes, there were other Owens in other companies, but she remembered Lana admitting that Owen was twenty years older than her, forty-five.

And here he was, smiling at her from his company's web page. Perfect hair, perfect teeth, perfect smile, and dark brown eyes, Abigail thought, that looked menacing.

'Owen Lyle, 45, managing director.'

'Got you, you bastard,' Abigail hollered.

The internet is a wonderful thing, and it was easy for Abigail to learn a lot about Owen Lyle. Through a little research, she found the apartment he used to have.

Taking the bull by the horns, Abigail drove south of the city to a quiet neighbourhood with smart houses along a tree-lined street and apartments overlooking a clean, well-looked-after park.

While she stood looking up at the apartment block Owen Lyle had lived in, a woman with shopping bags that looked ready to split stopped beside her.

'Are you looking for someone, dear?' The woman said, puffing as she put the bags down.

'Yes, I am. Do you live in this apartment block?'

'Why yes I do, dear, third floor.' The woman pointed.

'Did you know an Owen Lyle, by any chance?'

The woman laughed, taking Abigail by surprise. 'I take it that means you do?'

'I'm Mrs Harris; my apartment is above where Owen and Freya lived.'

'Freya?'

'Yes dear, his wife.'

'Well, well, this is becoming more and more interesting.'

'What is dear?'

'A dear friend of mine, Lana, has gone missing. She was seeing someone named Owen, and I've traced him to here.'

'Oh! You mean the young woman in the paper, blond hair, very pretty.'

Abigail nodded.

'Yes, I saw her come to the apartment a few times. I wasn't happy. I'll tell you that now.'

Mrs Harris looked at Abigail over the rim of her glasses. 'Does your friend usually date married men?'

'Mrs Harris, Lana wouldn't have touched this Owen if she'd known he was married. In fact, on the one time she told me about him, he'd told her he was a widower.'

'That doesn't surprise me, dear. Are you wanting to get in touch with Owen? Maybe ask him about your friend, Lana?'

'You have his new address?'

'Of course, dear. Help me with my shopping and I'll put the kettle on, make us a cup of tea. Then I'll tell you all about the questionable Owen Lyle.'

'Thank you, Mrs Harris. Mind if I take notes.'

'Of course not, dear. Make sure you get every detail down. I wouldn't want Owen Lyle to get away with how he treated Freya.'

'And my missing friend, Lana?'

Mrs Harris put a firm hand on Abigail's arm. 'Of course, my dear.'

CHAPTER 28

He'd decided to come home early from work. A migraine, he told Alan. The truth was, he couldn't think straight. All he could think about was the article in the newspaper, the one about the missing woman Alan had shown him yesterday.

It was a relief to him that Freya and Arthur were not home, and the handyman was nowhere to be seen.

In another part of his brain, this made him angry. What if the lout was with his wife, doing something he and Freya hadn't done in a long time?

Be intimate.

But right now, he only wanted to get his head down and rest for a couple of hours. Then he'd get the truth out of Freya and lover boy. No one, no one, messes with his wife but him.

Owen awoke abruptly and sat bolt upright in bed. His breath hurried. He wiped the sweat from his face. Blinking, he checked the time. The clock on the bedside table read 14:00.

He tugged off the covers and sat on the edge of the bed for a few minutes, trying to make sense of what had happened.

If only the thudding in his head would disappear as easily as… He stopped himself from completing the sentence.

Sloth-like, he made his way from the bedroom onto the landing. The light from the landing window always looked like dancing shadows to him

Owen shivered at the coldness and took a few steps.

'*Owen.*'

He rubbed his eyes.

'Owen.'

Something pulsated in front of him, coming closer, then retreating. Owen couldn't make what seemed to float above the floor, and he shook his head, trying to get his brain to understand what was in front of him.

In his half-sleep state, he stared at the soft hand that reached out to him.

His dry throat made it difficult for him to make a sound and he tried to swallow it away.

'La ...Lana?' He croaked.

'Owen, I miss you.'

The image came into focus, and Owen stumbled against the handrail.

'No, you can't be here. I made sure you were ...'

She cocked her head. *'Why not Owen? You brought me here, didn't you? I guess then it's your fault I'm here, isn't it?'*

Owen clung to the handrail. 'I'm dreaming. I've not been well, that's it, I'm hallucinating.'

'Are you Owen?' she came closer.

Owen gagged at the stench that filled his nostrils and spread down his throat.

A stench of decomposing flesh.

Panicked, he glanced over the handrail and down into the dark hallway. In his frantic, confused state, all he could think of was why was it dark in the afternoon. He scuttled away from the handrail. His body hit the wall, sending the table lamp smashing onto the floor. *'Are you going somewhere, Owen?'*

'No, go away.' he collapsed to the floor onto the smashed lamp and cried out as glass punctured his thigh.

Empty blue eyes stared down into his, and lank blond hair touched his face. Her face was so close to his that he could see and smell the decay of her, and he could also make out her anger.

Owen felt the bile in his stomach reach his mouth as the decomposing smell overcame him.

'*I'm still here.*'

Owen curled into a ball, his arms cradled his head, trying to hide from the hideous thing in front of him. His whole body trembled and sweat formed on his freezing skin.

'Owen?'

Hands grabbed at him.

'No, get off me, you bitch.' He flayed at the hands that were trying to grab at him.

'Owen, stop this.'

In his distant mind, he could hear a voice he recognised.

'Owen, it's me.'

With a shuddering intake of breath, Owen opened his eyes. Opened his bloodshot, terrified eyes.

'Bloody hell, Owen, what are you doing home? I thought you had a busy day ahead of you.'

Owen grabbed at her. 'Where the hell have you been?'

'Taking Arthur for a walk.' She pulled his hands off her.

Owen scrambled to his feet, steadying himself by clinging onto the handrail. His eyes glazed over as he stared at Freya.

'Are you okay? Are you sick because you look terrible?' Owen could only nod.

'I better clean this mess up before you get more shards stuck in you, ' she said calmly, ignoring the blood down his pyjama bottoms.

'Did you see her?' Owen mumbled, pointing behind his wife, as his eyes darted everywhere.

'See who? There's nobody here but us.' She stared at the man before her and felt a revulsion that surprised her.

Freya stomped down the stairs and headed to the kitchen, where she disposed of the shards of glass in the bin.

Hobbling and holding his bloody thigh, Owen followed her.
'It was so dark. I couldn't see a thing. And then she was here?'

'Okay, Owen, I'll humour you. Who was here?'

'She was here,' he sobbed. 'Lana.'

All Freya could do was stare at Owen, whose face looked pale, shocked, and... haunted. 'Lana? Why would the missing woman be here?' she felt her heart race.

'I ...I don't know.'

'I think you're overtired after reading about the missing woman in the paper. You've probably just had a nightmare. Come on, I'll help you back to bed.'

Freya silently guided him up the stairs, back into the bedroom, and covered him with the blankets.

Settled in the lounge, one of her first thoughts was that Owen had never left work early all the time she had known him because he was sick.

Second, why was he convinced he had seen the missing woman from the paper in their house? (she couldn't bring herself to call the house her home.)

And third, was Abigail right about her husband?

Since she had married Owen, her friends, the few friends she had before she'd met him, seemed to have dropped out of her life. Making excuses, they were busy or were moving too far away to visit.

They never wanted to be in Owen's company, although a few had hoped she was happy. But never happy for both of them, for her AND Owen.

Freya took another sip of coffee.

The house seemed quiet, apart from Arthur's gentle snoring after his long walk. Owen was in bed, exhausted from his nightmare. Sat on the sofa, she decided to look at her wedding album.

It had been a wonderful day. She stared at the smiling bride and groom, her and Owen. The witnesses had been Alan and his wife.

Freya stared hard at the picture. Something had always been in the back of her mind about Owen, and it had not really bothered her until now.

She really didn't know Owen Lyle at all.

Alan and his wife were the only people she'd met on his side.

When she worked at his advertising agency's office, she thought she had made some good friends.

Until she started dating Owen. In the blink of an eye, none of the other staff members seemed to want to talk to her.

Why?

Freya was, she had always thought, a cheerful, talkative person, interested in other people.

But others soon kept their distance.

Owen was more than attentive to her. He had taken her under his wing—in more ways than one. He didn't need to wine and dine her to seduce her into bed. She would have and did go willingly.

Alan had also welcomed her. He had a good sense of humour, as Freya found out when she thought Owen was Alan's boss.

Freya turned a few more pages of her wedding album. All the photos shared a common theme, and because she was so in love, it had never occurred to her. There were no guests—no one but her, Owen, Alan, and his wife.

Owen told her he was estranged from his family. They were jealous of his success, and he would tell her his family didn't have his drive, his ambition, or even savagery to get to the top. So he'd left them behind. No marks, he'd called them.

And here he was, on top of his game, in one of the best advertising agencies in the country.

Freya closed the album and went to the window.

What Abigail had told her earlier agitated her. Did Owen really have an affair with her friend Lana?

Abigail couldn't tell her much, only that Lana's boyfriend,

Owen, was named in Lana's diary, had a posh pad in Greystone Avenue and was the head of a top-class advertising agency.

There were three coincidences that Abigail told her that applied to Owen.

When Freya started as Owen's assistant, he was engaged to someone else. She knew this, but when he pursued her, she never gave his fiancé a second thought. Was Owen doing the same with Lana?

Freya shivered. She didn't know what to think, but the circumstances were unavoidable to miss.

Then, when she came home to find Owen delirious on the landing, saying he'd seen her, Lana, she'd felt physically sick.

CHAPTER 29

When he arrived at Blyneath House, and even though Freya had told him Owen had left for work early, Nathan was relieved to see Owen's car was gone. The last thing he wanted was to tell Freya about his find at the back of the house yesterday, with Owen breathing down his neck. He was wary about telling Freya as it was.

Nathan had only been working on the property for a few days, and now he stared at the object in front of him. He brushed his hand through his hair, baffled by the find and the obscure markings.

'Strange.' His voice fell flat in the chill of the late morning. He looked around him, and the slight breeze swayed the trees.

He'd mowed half the garden at the back of the house and had stopped when he discovered the object in front of him.

'Umm.' He touched the letter carved into the stone. 'Is that an E?'.

A loud snap from behind him made him jump in the silence, and he spun around and saw a mist swirl through the trees.

Nathan rubbed at his eyes, not sure what he had seen. Dreams of Freya had interrupted his sleep the last few nights.

They weren't pleasant dreams, as he would have liked. Freya was running, and he was running after her. Running from a dark figure.

Every time he got close to her to help her, he had a feeling of falling, and he would wake up with a jolt, his heart furiously pounding; he felt like he was going to have a heart attack.

He must be tired because he sure felt like he could fall asleep standing up. Nathan stared hard into the woods. The mist seemed to have disappeared; now, the only thing moving was the trees in the breeze. Taking a deep breath, he turned his attention back to the stone.

Nathan had heard about the tales of Blyneath House, about how strange things began to happen nearly twenty years ago.

Edward Blyneath, a rich man from somewhere up north. No one in the village was really sure where exactly had built the house after the war. Had made his money during WW2, ammunitions, so the talk of the village went.

Edward had had enough of the industrialised north, and, so the tale goes, with a flick of a coin, he came to Hartnell.

Edward had built the house and planted over 100 trees around it. But after his wife died after forty years, his heart wasn't in the place, and as he and his wife didn't have any children, he left, leaving it in the hands of the local solicitors for them to oversee the renting or selling of the place.

Not long after Edward left, a family moved in but decided it was too far out of the way and left within a year.

It had remained empty for two years after that. Soon, people who wanted to leave the rat race of the big cities decided it would be nice to live in the middle of nowhere. Some stayed for a few years, but after a while, one by one, families and couples would only stay at Blyneath for a couple of months and some only a few weeks.

They complained of a foul smell. Some said it was the worst smell they had ever had the misfortune to have invade their nostrils. No one could even guess where the stench was coming from. Some residents thought the place was cursed and no good had happened there.

Some even said it was the noises, the noises not just at night but during the day, creaks and bangs, and some even said they heard whispers, and when they'd come downstairs in the morning, doors would be open, cupboards would be open, and even chairs upturned A few had even been so scared they had fled in the middle of the night, leaving their belongings behind.

Owen and Freya Lyle were the latest owners. From what Freya had told Nathan, the strange happenings were starting again.

The front door opened. Freya appeared. 'Hi, Nathan. What are you waiting for?' she laughed across the driveway. 'Come on, you've got work to do.'

Nathan loved her laugh. It was uplifting.

'Checking for hidden rocks in the soil. It's next on my to-do list.' Nathan smiled.

What a lovely smile, Freya thought as she watched Nathan walk up to her. She held out the mug of hot tea to him.

'Thanks.' He took a few sips. 'Freya, can you come with me for a minute?' Nathan stood in front of her, a seriousness in his eyes.

'I've got something to show you.' He handed her his half-drunk mug of tea.

'What is it, Nathan?' Freya put both mugs of tea down on the ground.

'You know I've been cutting the overgrown grass round the back.'

Freya nodded.

'Well, I've found something, something I didn't expect to find.'

Freya couldn't fathom what he could have found to suddenly put him on edge. She followed him through the cut grass and almost bumped into him when he halted.

'I wasn't sure if I should show you. Didn't know if you got freaked out by things like this.' He stood aside to reveal a small headstone.

'Bloody hell. 'She bent down and brushed the debris away. 'There looks like an E and L I can't really tell as the letters are worn away.'

Nathan bent to look closer at the worn letters. 'An L?' he stared at the letters. 'But I only saw an E on the headstone when I found it yesterday.' He brushed his hand through his hair.

Freya controlled her desire to grab him and kiss him. 'What do you mean, you only saw an E on the headstone? It's pretty faded. Maybe you missed it, the L, I mean,' Freya said.

Stumped, Nathan said. 'Maybe.' But he knew what he saw. Or did he? After all, he thought he'd also seen a shadow in the woods yesterday. He wiped at the moss and dirt on the stone. He turned and headed back to the front of the house. 'I'll get on then. Try to uncover as many rocks as I can.' He didn't know what else to say.

Freya caught up with him. 'I guess making the house pretty on the outside might give me some incentive to make it pretty on the inside.'

Nathan stopped and looked at her. 'What? I've just shown you a headstone, and all you can think of is making this piece of shit into a home?'

Freya, astounded at Nathan's outburst, didn't know how to respond.

Nathan took hold of her hands. 'I'm so sorry. I didn't mean
to say that.'

Freya squeezed his hands. 'It's okay. It's my way of coping with something I don't like, ignoring it.'

He let go of her hands and suddenly felt his hands on her hips, gently pulling her toward him. His breath on her cheek as he bent and kissed her.

Oh, how she wanted him. Right here, right now.

She looked into his eyes and at the flush of his neck. The slight hardness against her thigh told her all she wanted to know.

But now was not the time.

In no time, Nathan had uncovered more than a dozen rocks and moved them to the side of the driveway so no vehicle would damage their undersides.

The sun began to set behind the trees. Freya watched as Nathan cleaned the gear and put them back in the outhouse.

The few hours between Nathan leaving and Owen returning home were growing all the time. Owen wouldn't be home for at least three hours.

She ran out into the driveway as Nathan got into his van and turned the engine on. 'Nathan, could you do me a favour?'

He turned off the engine, nodded and tried to keep his eyes off her cleavage as she leaned into the car.

'Could you stay longer? Owen won't be back for hours yet, and it creeps me out knowing about the headstone.'

'Sure. No problem.' Nathan got out of the van and followed Freya back into the house.

He hoped Owen wasn't on his way back, deciding to finish early.

Nathan wondered if Freya had another reason for him to stay with her. They had feelings for each other, and he knew they could easily go too far if given the chance.

Was this the chance Freya was hoping for?

Nathan thought to himself, what the hell was he doing? Freya had an innocence about her that made him want to care for her. Take her in his arms. He dismissed the thought.

The thought of them making love in her house, with Owen liable to arrive home anytime, changed his mind about staying.

Nathan didn't want Owen to have any reason to sack him because there was something about Owen Lyle that Nathan couldn't put his finger on.

But whatever it was, it was unpleasant.

What hurt him most was that he was certain Freya was hiding something from him or not telling him exactly what was happening behind the closed doors of Blyneath House.

And Nathan didn't want Freya to face whatever Owen was up to alone.

CHAPTER 30

The sun had set behind the trees when Owen stormed into the house, threw his briefcase onto the sofa, and headed to the smells from the kitchen.

'Freya, Freya.'

'What's with all the shouting?'

'What's going on, Freya?' Owen ignored her smile.

'I think I should ask you the same. What's going on with you?'

He pushed past her and glanced at the contents of the pot. 'What the hell, Freya? Making Spaghetti Bolognese – again.'

Freya watched as her husband got a spoon out of a drawer and tasted the sauce. But this time, his face screwed up, and he threw the spoon into the sink.

'Owen, what's wrong?' she grabbed his arm as he stormed past her.

He shrugged her hand off, headed for the stairs, and shouted.

'Nothing.' He stormed up two at a time.

Exasperated, she ran up the stairs after him and into the bedroom. 'I will not take that rudeness for an answer. Who the hell do you think you are talking to me like that? Had a bad day at the office, have you?'

She watched Owen pull off his tie and throw it, along with his suit jacket, on the bed. 'Sarcasm doesn't suit you, Freya. Okay, you really want to know. I passed that long-haired handyman on the road.

Working late, was he? I thought we'd agreed on the hours he'd work.' Freya, hands on hips, glared at him. 'He was not working late. You're home early, and how dare you insinuate something's going on between me and Nathan? Yes, I wanted him to stop later than normal, but he said he couldn't. I was a little scared of being on my own and when you messaged me telling me you'd be late back from work…again.'

Owen stopped mid-unbuttoning his shirt. 'What do you mean by again?'

Freya snorted and turned to leave the bedroom. 'Yeah, is that what you took from that statement, me getting on at you about working late again? Not the fact I was scared to be on my own.'

Before he could reply, she slammed the bedroom door behind her, leaving him to stare at the peeling old paint on the door he'd promised to repaint.

Back in the kitchen, Freya threw the contents of the pan into the bin. 'Sod him.' She said to Arthur, who was under the table, watching her intently.

The phone in the lounge rang, startling her. She wasn't in the mood to speak to anyone. 'Hello.'

'Mrs Lyle, it's Spud from the removal company you hired?'

'Oh, hello, Spud, what's up?'

'Umm….'

She heard him mutter something but couldn't make out the exact words.

'Spud, is there anything I can help you with?'

'Mrs Lyle, can I come and talk with you about not doing my job and why I wouldn't go into the house?' he coughed.

'Honestly, Spud, there's no need. This house still creeps me out even after being here for over a week, never mind the first day.'

'Really? Why?'

She sighed. 'Look, Spud, I really don't have time for this. I have enough on my plate with this damn house and then finding a headstone in the overgrown grass. It's not a good time.' Did she hear Spud take a sharp breath?

'Please, Mrs Lyle. It's really about my mum. I keep seeing her even though she left twenty years ago. I have a bad feeling, a really bad feeling something bad has happened to her.'

Freya put the phone down, annoyed with herself for caving into Spud and letting him come to see her.

It struck Freya as odd that Spud, who she only met that one day, wanted to talk to her about his missing mother.

What help could she give him? She remembered his uncle Eric saying he felt things.

Spud had sounded so desperate. She told him to come over tomorrow.

CHAPTER 31

In front of the house, Nathan hankered down to clear away the grass cuttings he'd dumped from the back garden. The day was chilly, and he had his hat pulled down when he heard footsteps on the gravelled driveway. He turned to see Spud walking up the drive. He had a book under his arm and looked very serious.

'Hey, Spud. What are you doing here?'

Spud said nothing, only waved at Nathan as he walked past. Amused, Nathan stopped what he was doing and watched Spud hesitantly knock on the front door and wait.

He heard a shout, 'Come in, it's open.'

Uncertain, Spud looked back at Nathan, then turned the doorknob and pushed the door open. Taking a deep breath, Spud stepped over the threshold of the house he knew was bad, maybe even scared of. He could feel his blood pressure rising, and he had to take deep breaths to calm himself before he stepped further into the hallway. He checked behind him at Nathan, who was still watching him. Tentatively, leaving the front door wide open, he headed towards the smell of baking.

Nathan knew Spud but had nothing much to do with him, except maybe the odd hello in passing. Spud and his uncle Eric mostly kept to themselves.

Nathan knew a little about Spud's past, about his mum leaving him and going wherever, and his dad passing two years later, leaving his uncle Eric to bring him up from twelve years old.

Why would Spud be seeing Freya?

Nathan could hear voices coming from the open window in the kitchen, but not exactly word for word, only making out the odd 'sorry', 'left' and 'help'.

He continued to put the cut grass into bundles, but kept pondering what the hell was going on.

Nathan shuddered and instinctively looked up at the top right corner window. There was no one looking down on him. No one shot away from the window.

But that didn't lessen the feeling he had in his stomach that something bad had happened in that room.

Yesterday, Nathan had to go into that room to fill the hole and paint the frame from the inside.

As soon as he entered the room, he felt a chill which seemed to seep into his bones. Warily he went to the window, put his tools on the floor, and got to work sanding the wooden frame.

Something made him stop what he was doing, his hand holding the sandpaper poised in mid-air.

For some unknown reason, a reason he couldn't explain, he felt the hairs on the back of his neck rise, and an uneasy sensation came over him.

He glanced over his shoulder, expecting to see someone standing in the doorway.

No one.

He tried to shake the feeling off and turned his attention back to his work.

Nathan still felt uneasy. Even though he was the only person in the room, he felt the presence of someone or something else. A heaviness overcame him, a sudden sadness, a feeling of being lost.

He straightened up and looked out of the window. His heart missed a beat. There, in the window's reflection, a woman stood behind him. Alarmed, he spun around.

No one.

He took a deep breath and turned back to the window. This time, the only reflection was his own.

As suddenly as the feelings of heaviness, sadness and of being lost had come over him, they lifted from him.

He finished the work quickly and haphazardly painted the repaired frame, then chucked his tools in his bag and grabbed his bag to leave.

Then he smelt it.

The scent of perfume, the smell of flowers, of roses.

Yes, he'd heard tales of the house. He'd lived in Hartnell all his life.

The house wasn't on a through or passing road, so you wouldn't go there unless you wanted to.

Many roads led away from Hartnell, but the only dirt track from the village led to the house.

Hearing voices coming from the open window brought Nathan back to today. He wondered what on earth Spud had to talk to Freya about. An apology, maybe?

He'd heard Spud's reluctance to go further than the front door threshold the day Freya and Owen had moved in.

CHAPTER 32

Spud had been gone for over four hours, and Eric's anxiety was getting the better of him. He felt sick to the stomach as he clenched and unclenched his clammy fists.

Eric sat at the kitchen table with the kitchen door wide open so he could see into the hallway. He willed the front door to open, but as the time dragged on, he felt his anxiety turning into anger.

'Why the hell would Spud go and see that Lyle woman?' he muttered into the quiet of the house.

Finally, for Eric, the front door creaked open, and Spud came into view. As soon as he saw Eric waiting for him in the kitchen, he said. 'I didn't go to apologise, Eric. I just wanted to talk to her.' he joined Eric at the kitchen table.

'What have you got there?' he pointed to the book Spud clutched in his hands.

'It's mine.'

Eric's gaze bore into Spud. 'I can see the way you hold it, it looks important to you, but that's not what I asked you. What have you got there?'

Spud's grip tightened around the book; his eyes were defiant. 'None of your business.'

Eric stood, hands splayed on the table, and leaned into Spud. 'Explain to me, Spud, so help me. I'll whip your damn behind.' he raised his fist at Spud. 'Why did you go and see the Lyle woman without telling me first so you could rehearse what you needed to say?'

Spud scraped back his chair and stood. 'You even try to whip me, old man, and I'll knock you out so cold you'd never get back up.' 'What…' Eric spluttered, totally stunned. 'Don't talk to me like that, boy!'

'I already did.' Spud had never talked back at his uncle like that before, even though there had been many times he'd wanted to.

His conversation with Freya had ignited something in him.

He felt an energy, a sense of worth, a strength he had never felt before.

Standing up to his uncle gave Spud the confidence and courage to find the answers he desperately sought.

No matter who stood in his way.

As he left the kitchen, Spud turned to Eric. 'Night.'

Eric heard Spud's hard footsteps on the stairs, and his bedroom door slammed shut. Shakily, he hobbled to the kitchen sink and looked out the window at the back garden, full of years of rubbish piled up and full of items he would fix up and eventually sell to earn money. Eventually.

Other people might call his garden full of junk, but it wasn't to Eric.

It was a way out of this dump he had had to call home for the last twenty years. The place was full of terrible memories he just wanted to escape from, leave behind, and not have to look at the woods in the distance that reminded him of the madness of that night.

Of all the lying to, well, to everybody. Especially Spud.

It pained Eric to lie, but what had happened wasn't his fault. Seth had escaped all the lying by drinking himself selfishly into an early grave. Eric, deep down, was glad, though. Seth had ruined his life and flaunted his prize in front of him every single day.

That prize was Rose.

When Spud came into the world, that was the last straw. Eric decided then to move away. He couldn't take it anymore.

Watching his Rose, with Spud and his older gloating brother, Seth.

Seth had been dead for these last 18 years, and Eric was still lying for him.

'She ran away, Spud. That's all. She ran away from your dad.

She couldn't handle all the housewife mum stuff,' Eric said to his reflection in the window as he recalled the conversation with Spud after his mum had left.

Eric stifled a sob.

Now, everything was falling apart.

Everything had changed since the Lyles had moved into Blyneath, and it was all down to one person.

As for Spud, what had got into the lad? And what the hell had that Freya woman said to him to make him so......determined?

He'd always known how upset and frustrated Spud had been, not knowing where his mum was. And his talk of seeing her, once on the front lawn and another time around the corner of the house, was disturbing.

Eric wondered if he should have a word with this Freya. Maybe get her to have another chat with Spud. Get him to drop everything about his mum, make him realise he'd just been dreaming or hallucinating because he missed her so much.

Because if she couldn't, he'd be in big trouble.

Because if she couldn't, her husband's lies would be exposed.

CHAPTER 33

Tap! Tap! Tap! The sound wouldn't let go.

Owen shot his wife a look, but she was sleeping peacefully beside him, albite on the edge of the bed. After their argument yesterday, when he had come home earlier than expected and accused her of being with Nathan, they hadn't spoken more than half a dozen words to each other, which was okay with him. He was in no mood to talk to anyone, let alone his wife.

Tap! Tap! Tap!

There it was again, louder this time.

Tap! Tap! Tap!

Owen swung his feet onto the cold floor, sat on the edge of the bed, and struggled to listen for the sound again.

Nothing. Had he dreamt it?

He glanced back at his wife and was incredulous. How on earth did she not hear the tapping? Rubbing his eyes, he wondered if he had actually heard anything.

The stress at work was wearing him down, and the constant chit-chat from the office staff about the missing girl and their side-sly looks gave him a headache.

No, it was giving him nightmares. Nightmares he deserved.

Did he? No, he thought. It was not his fault what happened to Lana Young.

Owen stared at the bedroom door. He didn't want to discover what was making the tapping sound, the alleged tapping sound he had heard.

He took a deep breath, trying to calm himself as the memory of the image he had seen a few days ago burst into his brain.

The look on Freya's face when she had found him curled up in a ball on the landing, whimpering. It was a look he would never forget or forgive her for.

A look of total disdain and disgust rolled into one toward him.

But the tapping, the noise from the other side of the bedroom door, was getting into his head. He had to make sure no one was waiting for him on the landing.

Unsure about leaving the bedroom, he finally inched towards the door while continually checking behind him to see if Freya was still asleep.

When he opened the door, it creaked slightly, a noise he'd not noticed before.

The lamp on the small side table under the landing window was the only light, and its dim glow looked like shadow fingers stretching out to him. He glanced out of the window above the lamp.

The face in the window shocked him. The pale face and haunting eyes of his reflection stared back at him.

'Shit.' Owen gasped, seeing his chilly breath hit the window. He grabbed the handrail and squinted down into the darkness below, then felt his way along, making a mental note to up the wattage of the bulb in the lamp on the landing.

'Hello.' He felt like an idiot as his voice filled the empty air.

He counted each step from the top of the staircase until he reached the bottom. '13, unlucky for some,' he snorted.

'Hello.' He whispered again, not knowing what to do if there was a reply.

'*It's really dark down here.*'

Owen's breath stopped. He felt his chest tighten as he tried to take deep breaths.

Eventually, he exhaled, which sounded like a hurricane inside his head, and absentmindedly took his right hand off the handrail to wipe the sweat away with the sleeve of his pyjamas. His neck felt hot and clammy, and as he stroked his neck, a coolness came over him. He jolted as a soft touch stroked the side of his face.

He grabbed the handrail and turned in a panic. 'Who's there?' '*Remember Me?*'

Owen recognised the voice. Panicked, he staggered back to his bedroom, his hands shaking in front of him as he clawed at the sudden darkness around him, not able to see where he was going.

With a sigh of relief, his hand found the bedroom door, and he opened it as quietly as his shaking body would allow.

Before closing it behind him, he forced himself to glance back out onto the landing.

All he could see was darkness.

All he could smell was roses.

CHAPTER 34

Freya was getting used to walking to the village to stock up on a few items. She felt it did her good, giving her a bit of time to think about things. And the bonus, she thought, was Arthur loved the walk too.

She dumped the shopping on the kitchen table, removed her coat, and slung it over a chair. From a kitchen drawer, she took out a picture of a woman. Spud had given her the picture of his mum when he had visited yesterday.

She recalled what Spud had said to her. 'I think it was about 20 years ago. I would have been about ten. Not long after that, she left after an argument with my dad,' Tears had welled up in the corner of his eyes.

She didn't want to upset him anymore, but asked him, 'When you see your mum, what does she look like?'

The question caught Spud off guard. It was something he'd not thought of. 'Like in the picture, I guess.'

Freya touched his arm gently and smiled. 'Maybe what you're seeing is actually what I'd call a sighting. Being able to see spirits. Although I'm not a believer,…'

Spud slumped in the chair and put his head in his hands. 'I'm sorry to burden you with all this about me.'

Freya patted his arm. 'No need to be sorry, honest.'

'I knew she wasn't real. I knew I was seeing her…what you said…her spirit. But my uncle made it out that I was dreaming and all that. But I know what I saw, what I kept seeing. The dreams were fading, but then you moved in and… and my dreams got more intense than before. It's like she's trying to tell me something.'

Freya looked deep into Spud's eyes. 'Spud, what do you think your mum is trying to tell you?'

'Something bad has happened here in your

house.' Perplexed, Freya said. 'Bad, in my

house?' Spud nodded.

'Bad what, exactly?' She didn't want to disclose to Spud what had been happening in her house. She couldn't understand it herself.

'Well, I remember Eric was upset at the picture of the young woman, you know, the one who's missing.'

'Lana Young.' Freya sat back in the chair and tried not to let the name jolt her. 'Does your uncle know anything about her disappearance?'

'What do you mean, her disappearance? Why would Eric know anything about the missing woman in the paper? Anyway, when I ask Eric about Mum, he shrugs. But then, in the next breath, he says she was like a sister to him and wouldn't let any harm come to her.'

He shrugged. 'What am I supposed to think of that?'

'Why didn't you want to come into the house the day we moved in?'

Spud looked down at his hands. 'I saw a shadow. It swirled, and I couldn't make it out. It was too dark to see details, but...' he trailed off.

'Spud, you think it was your mum in the shadows, here in my house?'

147

'I don't know. But don't you think it's crazy? My dreams have been stronger since you and Mr Lyle moved into Blyneath. I mean, they were subsiding, like I said.'

'I don't know how I can help you, Spud, but I'm here if you need to talk some more.'

He couldn't help himself; he leaned across the table and hugged her. 'Thank you for listening to me.'

Freya hugged Spud back and lifted a hand to Nathan, who had entered the kitchen.

'Everything okay?' Nathan asked.

Spud stood and picked up the photo album he'd brought with him. 'You can borrow my mum's picture, just in case.'

Nathan patted Spud's shoulder as he passed him, then sat on the chair Spud had just vacated and picked up the photo.

'Will you be able to help Spud?' he asked, eyeing Freya as she watched Spud walk down the driveway and disappear.

'I don't know how, I really don't. He just wants someone to talk to. To believe he is feeling something. And he's obviously so confused and upset about how his mum just left him. I think he just misses her. And until he faces up to the fact that his mum's probably dead, he'll never feel better.

'Can I give you a bit of advice, Freya?' She turned to him.

'Be careful. I've lived in the village all my life. I kind of know Spud. His actual name is Michael. Now and then, the question of how his mum just up and left comes around. Spud gets upset, obviously, and he can get clingy. And you helping him, letting him talk, he may start being clingy toward you.'

'What does that mean, Nathan?'

'What I'm trying to say is, Spud might not be all there.' Nathan tapped the side of his head.

'Is he dangerous? Has he hurt people?'

'Not as far as I know.'

'Well then, that's just hearsay, isn't it? I don't know Spud like some do around here, but I do know that he is hurting. Not just by his mum leaving, but also how his uncle Eric treats him.'

Nathan stood. 'I think it's time I finished for the day.'

Freya could have kicked herself for speaking so sharply to Nathan. She could tell her harsh words had hit him by the crushed look on his face.

Freya put the photo of Spud's mum back in the drawer.

She hoped Nathan was only looking out for her. The idea that Nathan could care about her in that way made her tingle.

She was sure there was something between them. When they touched or looked at each other, something was there; she could feel it—the touch of their hands, the shiver she felt when he looked at her.

Then she looked down at her wedding ring.

What if what she had been told was true?

Both anger and sadness hit her all at once.

CHAPTER 35

'Open up.' Abigail banged on the front door. 'I know you're in there. I saw you.' She stepped back to scour up at the top windows. There was no one, nothing. She glanced at the bottom window to her left and decided to have a peek. Standing on tiptoes, Abigail saw it was the kitchen. It was empty.

'Damn.' She sneaked around to the back garden and stood facing the back of the house. 'Shit, how eerie this place looks.'

The back windows seemed to look down on her with dead, dark eyes. The middle window looked back at her.

'Hay, I can see you, Owen,' The eyes quickly disappeared. 'I want to talk to you.'

The sensation of warmth on the back of her neck, like a breath, startled her. She spun around. No one was there. She was alone.

The sun disappeared behind a cloud, and the air chilled. The trees swayed, and the leaves rustled as if whispering a secret.

Rubbing her neck, Abigail looked around her and noticed her surroundings for the first time. Part of the grass had recently been cut, and in the distance, in the growing dimness of the late afternoon sky, she could make out a slab of stone.

Abigail glanced back at the house and debated whether to leave or check out the stone. The stone won.

As she approached the stone, she saw a movement in her peripheral vision to her left. Turning around, she could only see the darkness creeping through the woods.

Her brain told her to leave, but Abigail was curious.

She headed toward the stone and shivered at the sudden low temperature. 'Shit. A headstone.'

She couldn't move. Her mind whirled with the thought of Lana. 'Please don't be.'

Abigail leaned into the stone, her brows furrowed. 'What the?' She took her phone out of her coat pocket and, with the flashlight on, took a couple of photos. Standing back, she couldn't help but stare at the headstone. A chill wind caught her hair and swirled it around her face. As she brushed her hair away, she glanced up at the top floor of the house again, then, for no reason, into the woods behind her.

Abigail hurried back to the front of the house and banged on the front door again. 'I'm not finished with you, Owen Lyle. I have all the proof I need in Lana's own words, in her handwriting.'

The noise of hurried footsteps down a wooden staircase startled her, and she ran to her car.

Hands shaking, she pulled open the car door and jumped in.

After a few panicked attempts, the engine caught, and she turned the car around in the driveway.

In her rearview mirror, Abigail gasped at the hand gripped around the semi-open front door.

Owen couldn't take the banging and shouting anymore. He crawled to the front window of his bedroom and glanced at the woman angrily searching the windows.

Quickly, he ducked down, hands on the windowsill, his head leaned against the cold, cracked wall underneath the window.

'I know you're in there.' The woman's voice pierced his brain.

He wished she would go away. Or he could make her go away.

He peeked out the window again just in time to see the woman head for the back garden.

Scurrying on his hands and knees, he crawled from his bedroom to the landing window and peered out to see the woman staring up at him.

But she wasn't alone.

A shaking hand shot up to his mouth to stop the bile that had settled in his throat from pouring out.

'No, no.' he shook his head as the two women looked up at him.

There she was, the second woman, with a sneer on her face, her hair lank, and her skin grey. With dead eyes, she glared at him.

He could see her breath touch the woman's neck like a breath on a cold glass pane.

'No!' Owen stammered. 'No.'

The woman, startled, rubbed the back of her neck and then took in the view around her.

Owen couldn't hold in the bile any longer. He threw up on the landing carpet; sweat poured down his back. His whole body shook as he pulled himself up and forced himself to peek out of the landing window again.

The woman who shouted at him had found something else to interest her. He watched her peer at a stone and then take a photo with her phone.

The banging on the door and the shouting started again.

Owen lay there, paralysed, his limbs betraying him. Fear gripped him at the sound of heavy footsteps on the staircase. His brain whirled with dread at who or what was in his house.

CHAPTER 36

Eric sat on the sofa, his back straight and jaw tense. Not knowing what was happening gave him heartburn, and he didn't like heartburn. He always thought the next step was going to be a heart attack. He felt anger at what he's been forced to do. Not once, but twice.

Every day, Eric cursed Seth for calling him in the middle of the night, out of breath, and whispering that Rose had had a terrible accident and could he come quickly to help.

'What can I do, Seth? You need to call the doctor if she's badly hurt.'

Seth growled down the phone. 'I can't.'

Eric had jumped in his car, and even after two beers and a glass of whiskey, he would have driven anywhere for Rose. Seth could go to hell as far as he was concerned.

Fifteen minutes later, he pulled up outside the house.

Seth was waiting for him outside. Eric gingerly got out of his car, wrapping his coat around him against the icy rain of the night.

'What the hell, Seth? Look at the state of you. What's happened and where's Rose?'

Seth grabbed him by the arm and dragged him back to his car.
'We need to drive around the corner, away from the house and prying eyes.'

'Seth, what you are talking about?'

Seth got in Eric's face. 'Eric…. I did something bad.'

Shaking, Eric got back into his car with a panicked Seth in the passenger seat and drove along the road until he reached the start of the field and the woods above.

'Stop here.' Seth stumbled out of the car before it stopped and stood looking across the field. He turned to Eric. 'Come on. She's over there.' Seth pointed toward the top left corner of the field.

Standing beside his brother, Eric squinted into the darkness, trying to make out Rose.

'She's over there, Eric.' Seth headed for the top left corner of the field. Eric followed him, still struggling to make out Rose.

'How badly is she hurt?'

'You'll see.'

Suddenly, Seth stopped and blurted out. 'She's dead, Eric, she's dead. She hit her head when she fell. I tried to wake her, but she wouldn't wake up.'

'What?' Eric scoured Seth's face into his eyes. 'She's dead?' Eric felt the beer and whiskey rising in his throat.

The sudden calmness in Seth's face and his dry eyes worried Eric. 'What have you done, Seth?'

'Nothing.'

Eric grabbed his arm. 'You better tell me the truth, or I'm leaving.'

'Let's get her.' Seth shrugged Eric's hand off.

Eric tried to grab Seth's arm again but missed. He lagged after Seth as he waded across the wet grass.

Seth stopped.

'No.' Eric gasped at the sight of a lifeless Rose lying sprawled on the grass, the rain bouncing off her.

'We have to put her somewhere. Somewhere no one will find her.'

'No, Seth. You have to go to the police. Explain how it was an accident.' Eric paused. 'It was an accident, wasn't it?'

'I can't.'

'Why the hell not?'

'Police won't believe it was an accident, with her black and blue from beatings I give her.'

Eric stared at his brother. A mist came over him and he punched Seth square on the jaw.

Seth staggered backwards. 'I deserved that.' He rubbed his jaw.

Eric clenched his fits again. He so wanted to beat the crap out of Seth. But Rose was lying dead a few yards in front of them.

As he approached Rose, Eric felt he was going to collapse.

The sight of her just lying there motionless brought uncontrolled tears.

He knelt next to her, took her lifeless hand in his, and kissed it. The weight of grief hit him like lightning. His body racked with hate and rage at the sight of Rose, left like a bag of manure.

The heavy rain splattered her hair over her face, and Eric gently wiped her hair away.

'You're wearing your favourite dress, Rose, pink with little flowers on. It's my favourite too, Rose.'

Eric laid his head on her chest and looked down at her splayed legs.

He shot a look at Seth, who stared expressionless at Rose, his hands in his pockets and the rain bouncing off his shoulders.

Reluctantly, Eric let go of Rose's hand and stood to face his brother. 'What else have you done to Rose?'

Seth stepped away from his brother.

'What else have you done to Rose?' he yelled, his voice almost inaudible in the strengthening wind and rain.

Seth put his hands up in a defence position. 'Eric, I swear she was alive when we had sex.'

Seth knew it was coming but was too slow to react when Eric's fist hit him square on the jaw for the second time. He staggered backwards, arm flaying, trying to keep his balance and not fall in the muddy grass.

'I deserved that one as well, Eric.' Seth rubbed at his swelling jaw.

Eric clenched his fists again.

'Come on, Eric, we need to take her somewhere, somewhere no one will find her.'

'Why the hell should I help you, Seth? Give me one good reason why I shouldn't go to the police?'

'Because if you go to the police, Eric, they will charge you with helping me. Both of us will end up in the nick. What would happen to Spud then, eh?'

Eric's emotions swirled as the rain masked his tears. He wanted so badly to stand up to his older brother.

An older brother who had continually teased and bullied him when he was growing up. Telling Eric he was worthless and that he, Seth, was going to be the one to make their parents proud by joining the army and travelling the world.

And Seth did that for a while until his temper got the better of him one drunken night when he got into a fight.

He was discharged from the Army without honours. Of course, only Eric knew this side of Seth, and Seth threatened him with his life if he told anyone.

Eric cursed himself as he helped Seth take hold of Rose. He thought Rose deserved so much better than being buried in the dirt like rubbish.

The front door opened, bringing Eric back to his current reality. 'Spud, that you? I've got the kettle on if you want a brew,' he said, facing the open kitchen door like he always did when waiting for Spud to come home.

'No, thanks, I'm all brewed up.' Spud turned to go up to his room.

Eric was about to say something but changed his mind. He didn't want to say anything out of order.

Eric prayed that his nephew never found out what really happened the night he thought his mum had left him.

Every time Eric closed his eyes, he saw what he had done and what he had been forced to do.

And Owen Lyle only made things worse.

CHAPTER 37

Owen sat in his car and gripped the steering wheel, taking a few deep breaths to calm his nerves. Only a couple of other cars were in his company's car park.

What the hell does Alan want? he thought. In all his years working at the company, Alan's secretary had never summoned him to come into work on a Saturday for a meeting with the CEO, Alan Unsworth.

Usually, it was Alan who called him personally about any meetings

Owen and Alan had joined the advertising company so many years ago, when their hair was still something to be proud of and the lines on their faces far, far away, and had clawed, schemed and trodden on many people to get to the top. And when the company came up for sale, Alan jumped at the chance and bought it.

Owen was really pissed at Alan. No, he was angry at Alan for not giving him the opportunity to join him and buy the company together.

But Alan was true to his word and made Owen second in command of the entire company.

One day, Owen was certain he would be the next CEO.

Wait! Was this it? Was Alan retiring, and he was next in line for the CEO position?

That must be it. Everything had to be legitimate, so Alan had his secretary call him to make the appointment.

He sighed with relief and got out of his car, opened the back passenger door, and grabbed his suitcase and suit jacket.

Standards had to be kept, even on a Saturday.

The building seemed eerily quiet. There were usually a few people milling about, even at the weekend, finishing deadline work or getting a head start on the next deadline.

The reception area was always manned, but there seemed to be no one around this Saturday.

Owen turned at the sound of echoing footsteps coming from the far end of the lobby. A security guard was heading his way.

'Can I help you, sir?' the security guard said, his voice booming in the quiet reception area.

'Er...I'm Owen Lyle. Mr Unsworth requested I come in for a meeting with him today.'

'I see. Just one moment, sir, I'll call his office to let him know you're here.'

'Thank you, Mr...?'

'Monty Willis, I'm the weekend security guard these days. New to the job, so if you'll excuse me, Mr Lyle.'

Owen watched as Monty Willis swaggered to the empty reception desk, lifted a phone, and punched in a few numbers.

'Mr Unsworth, Mr Lyle is here for your meeting.' Pause. 'Okay, thank you Mr Unsworth, I'll show him up.'

As Monty Willis walked to the lift, Owen lifted his hand. 'It's okay. You don't have to escort me. I know the way.'

Monty pressed the button for the top floor before Owen could. 'No can do, Mr Lyle. Got to follow orders.'

The tinny music coming into the lift saved the two men from the awkward silence while riding to the top floor.

Owen didn't bother to protest as he walked behind Monty
Willis, right up to the CEO's office door. He let him knock, wait for a come-in, and then open the door to let Owen pass. The office blinds were half down.

'Thanks for the escort, Monty Willis.' Owen tried to sound sincere, but the look on Monty Willis's face as he closed the office door saw he'd failed.

'Alan, hello?'

Owen set his briefcase down by the chair.

'Sit down, will you, Owen? I'm just making us a coffee,' said Alan from a small room beside his office.

A few moments later, Alan came through with two cups of coffee and set them down on the coasters.

'Thanks for coming in on a Saturday, Owen.' Alan settled into his chair opposite him.

'It's not a problem, Alan. I'm curious about this meeting, especially since all the staff appear to be absent, apart from Monty Willis. He told me he was the new security guard.

'Yes, he's a good lad.'

Owen shifted in his chair and looked across the table at Alan.
'So, what do you want to talk about, Alan? What's so important it couldn't wait until Monday. Is it to do with your impending retirement and the vacancy it will leave?'

Alan sighed and brushed his hands through his thinning hair.

161

'No.' he pulled a newspaper out from his desk drawer. 'It's about this.' He shoved the paper across his desk. Owen leaned in to see what Alan was talking about.

Owen felt his heart drop to his stomach as he grabbed the paper and stared at the picture of the young woman on the front page. 'Why…. why…is this what you've called me into the office for? A picture of some missing woman on the front page? The same woman we talked about the other day.'

Alan placed his elbows on the table and glared at Owen.

'We both know she wasn't just any woman, don't we, Owen?'

'What? Why am I here, Alan?'

'I think you know exactly why you're here. Keep reading,

Owen. It's very interesting. Oh, and read it out loud.'

Owen, in total disbelief, read. 'Abigail Hall told this publication her missing friend, Lana Young, had a boyfriend, a secret boyfriend. She is certain Lana didn't tell her much about him, on his say so, because he was married. Abigail had no time for the likes of men who cheated on their wives. He was an older man. No doubt troubled about getting caught and so got rid of her. And her baby.'

Owen swallowed. 'Alan?' He glanced up at his boss and friend, who scowled at him. 'This is a load of shit.'

'Really?'

'Well, if you think I'm the secret boyfriend, you're very much

out of it, Alan.'

'Why? The past tells a different story, Owen.'

'Yes! I can prove I've not been having an affair…with anyone.'

'Oh, why do you need to prove it, Owen?'

Owen abruptly stood. 'Why are you accusing me?'

Alan calmly walked around his desk and sat on the side of it. 'I have someone in the back there,' he pointed to where he'd been making coffee for them both. 'Who can verify, categorically, that you were having an affair?'

Owen felt the rush of blood to his face and neck, and he wiped his sweaty hands down his trousers. He stared open-mouthed and bugged-eyed at the kitchen's entrance.

As soon as she came into the office, holding her baby bump, he screamed.

He could hear screaming in his head, the noise guttural, and hands on him, shoving him as he tried to push away.

'Owen, wake up.'

In the distance, he heard his wife calling his name. The screaming left his head, and he opened his eyes to see his wife's angry face looking down at him.

Owen grabbed hold of his wife.

'What are you playing at, Owen? Stop it, for your sake and everyone else. Especially Abigail.'

Freya felt Owen stiffen his grip.

'Abigail?' He took his arms from around her and grabbed for her hands. 'Abigail?'

Freya struggled to pull her hands away, but Owen squeezed her hands harder.

'You know this, Abigail? From where?'

She pulled harder and freed her hands from Owen's grasp.

'Owen, Lana, the missing woman, her friend? She must be frantic.'

'How the hell would you know this Abigail would be frantic?'

'From the paper, that's all.' Freya inched away from Owen.

'Really?'

'Of course. Come on, Owen. It's her best friend who's missing; if this Abigail isn't frantic about where she is, then she's not much of a friend, is she?'

Freya could hear the pounding of her heart in her ears, and she felt she could pass out any minute.

The only thing keeping her on her feet was the look of doubt in Owen's eyes. The look of suspicion in them. She had to deflect his question.

'Do you know Lana's friend Abigail?

Freya leaned against the wardrobe for support and glanced at the bedroom door. Owen stood between her and her getaway route.

He reached out his hand and stroked her hair. Fearful he would grab her hair and pull her down, Freya pushed his hand away.

'Don't touch me.'

Owen sighed and sat on the bed, never taking his eyes off her. 'Go on then, the door's there.' he pointed toward the closed door.

'Whatever you think of me, whatever you think I've done,

164

I'm sorry.' Then tears flowed.

Freya sat beside him on the bed and reluctantly played the part of the caring wife.

'I'm sorry too.' She put an arm around his shoulders.

'It's just I'm under so much stress at work, and I really don't know why I keep having these fucking nightmares about somebody I don't know.'

'It must be hard for you. I understand more than you think.'

Owen looked at her. 'What do you mean by that?'

She shrugged and headed for the door and, with her hand on the handle, turned to face her husband. 'Nothing. I know how hard you work, that's all.'

Outside on the landing, Freya leaned against the bedroom door. Thoughts of her husband having sex with the missing woman took over her, and the anger and disdain she felt toward Owen was becoming harder to hide.

But she thought as she stared down the landing at the closed door at the far end, why did she believe someone she had never met over her husband of three years?

CHAPTER 38

Exasperated by Owen, Freya had left him to rest for a few hours. But now she leaned against the kitchen sink, a warm cup of tea in her chilly hands, and looked over the cup's rim. Her gaze settled on Owen as he paced restlessly up and down the length of the kitchen while he ran his hands through his greasy hair.

'It was so vivid,' Owen said, his eyes red from lack of sleep.

'Some nightmares are. Just sit down and don't think about it.'

Owen stopped pacing in front of his wife and searched her eyes for the smallest of empathy. 'You believe me, don't you, Freya?' 'I don't know.'

Stunned, Owen snapped. 'What the hell is that supposed to mean? I don't know?'

'Well, there's a missing woman. You have a dream about her. And not for the first time, so you told me, which is disturbing in itself if you've never met her.'

'I don't know her and have never met her,' Owen insisted. His frustration was simmering at the surface. He had to stay calm and not say anything that would alert Freya he was not telling the truth. He forced his thoughts to stop.

'Nightmares. Why? That's my nagging thought, Owen. Why?' she sipped her tea. 'You don't even know the woman. Do you?' she repeated.

Owen looked away from her intense gaze and continued to pace up and down the kitchen.

Freya put her cup in the sink and stopped him, grabbed his chin, and forced him to look at her. 'Owen, you don't know the woman, do you? Tell me the truth; that's all I ask from you.' she let go of his face, but her mistrust hung in the air.

Unexpectedly, Owen burst out laughing. 'You should have seen your face. I'm only messing with you; of course, I don't know her.'

'Don't mess with me, Owen. Something's not right here. Your nightmares about hearing voices…'

'Hang on, you've been having nightmares, too.'

'I prefer to call them strange dreams. Brought on by the stress of this damn forced move.' I think there's something in the woods out front. Something that's causing us to have dreams and nightmares.' She stared hard at Owen. 'Don't you think so? What could be in the woods, Owen?' She searched his face, waiting for something to register.

Owen couldn't look at her. 'I don't know. Why should I?'

'I know it's been a stressful time for both of us. But these nightmares have to stop and I'm going to get to the bottom of them.'

Owen frowned at her. 'What are you implying?'

'Should I be implying something?' Freya paused. 'Anyway, I'm not implying anything. Just something's not right. Remember when I told you I went into the woods after Arthur's ball because he wouldn't fetch it? Well, I felt…' she shivered at the memory, 'I felt I was being watched.'

Freya studied Owen's now agitated face.

'Don't be silly. If someone were in the woods, we'd know

about it.'

Freya shoved past him. 'How would we know? In our dreams?' From the hallway, Freya shouted. 'I'm going to get Nathan to investigate the woods, see if there are any signs of someone sleeping rough or whatever else is in there.' Freya's voice drifted into the distance as she disappeared up the stairs.

As Freya's footsteps faded, Owen fell against the kitchen cupboards and pressed a hand to his chest. The pain was getting worse by the day. 'I can't take this any longer.' He whimpered. 'I have to do something to stop this.'

He glanced over his shoulder at the woods and, not for the first time, had wished he'd kept his temper in check.

It took all his strength to open the front door, and, with a deep breath, he stepped outside.

A brush against his leg startled him until he realised it was Arthur doing his usual trick of running to the back of the house to do his business.

The sunlight filtered through the woods like shadows that danced amongst the trees.

Standing there, unable to move, he felt the trees closing in, their long branches reaching for him, wanting him.

Wanting him to come closer.

CHAPTER 39

After a frosty day of a truce between Freya and Owen, she was glad Nathan returned the next day. As soon as she opened the front door, Arthur bounded outside and headed to the back of the garden.

'Why does he do that?' Nathan asked. 'Why does Arthur always go around the back of the house when there is a perfectly good place right there?' Nathan pointed to the woods directly opposite the house as his other hand touched hers.

'He doesn't like that part of the woods. When we first came here, he ran off in that direction but halted in his tracks, started barking, and ran back out again. Never been in there since. Although he will sometimes just sit and bark from the front door.'

'Humm. Some people think dogs can sense things we can't— strange things beyond our sight, even our hearing.'

'Talking about sensing things, I'm glad, sort of, that you had the foresight not to come into the house the other night. It turns out Owen was already on his way, and I don't know what he would have seen.'

Nathan turned to face her, taking her face in his hands, his lips so close to hers. Freya felt the gentle softness of his lips, felt like her legs were going to give way, and she could feel the heat of his body against hers.

Arthur came bounding back around, headed for Freya, when he suddenly swerved, headed for the part of the woods he hated, and sat and barked.

The moment was gone. Nathan and Freya reluctantly let go of each other.

'Arthur, come here.' as she took hold of his collar, a motion caught her eye. She pulled him away.

'Hello.' She called.

Nathan was next to her in an instant. 'You see someone? Are you all right, Freya? You've gone pale?'

She steered Arthur back into the house. 'I'm not sure. I thought I did. Actually, Nathan, I was going to ask you to check the woods out to see if someone is living rough, maybe. Something is going on around here, and I don't like it.'

Nathan quickly hugged her. 'I'll have a quick look.'

'Be careful.'

Nathan cautiously headed into the woods. He stood for a while, squinting, as his eyes adjusted to the semi-darkness.

His footsteps crunched on fallen leaves and rotting vegetation as he shoved tree branches aside from his face. 'Damn it,' he muttered under his breath. Twelve feet in, he stopped and looked around. 'Why does this place give me the creeps?' he thought. The image of the woman in the small room invaded his thoughts, and he forced himself not to think about it. Not here, not in these dark, uninviting woods. The further in he went, the colder the air got, and the light seemed to fade as darkness enclosed around him.   And the smell was like nothing he'd ever smelt before. Yes, he knew the smell of rotting undergrowth and animals that roamed through the woods and died, but this smell was different. It was putrid. And it went deep up his nostrils and down his throat.

He stepped to the right to avoid a fallen tree trunk and looked down at the ground to see if a dead animal was where the smell was coming from. The stench was so bad it was making him gip.

His gaze rested upon turned soil, which looked out of place with the rest of the forest floor. He stepped towards the mound. Not realising he was holding his breath, when he exhaled he made himself jump.

Nathan knelt beside the mound. A shiver ran down his spine as he considered what could be buried under the earth.

'Bloody hell.' He pinched his nose and felt a churning in his stomach as the stench increased around him. 'Sod this.' He looked around the quietness of the woods, the unnatural quietness that unnerved him.

Nathan decided to head back to Freya, but he couldn't help himself and took one more look back at the freshly turned-over soil. Something shiny caught his eye, gleaming in the little light that reached the forest floor. He leaned in and noticed part of what looked like a ring.

But the dankness and the strong rotting smell emanating from the ground made him only want to get out.

As he stepped back into the sunshine, Freya asked. 'Did you see anything?'

'No. It might have been an animal you saw before, and it was probably more scared of you. You probably scared it off.'

Freya tried to sound convinced. 'You're right,' she said, and returned to the house.

Nathan followed her with a glance over his shoulder. Something was hiding.

He could feel it, just like the feeling he had in the small room at the top of the house. It disturbed him.

CHAPTER 40

Owen listened to the sound of footsteps behind him. Was this another case of his imagination?

Slowly, he turned, fingers unconsciously crossed, not wanting to see the emptiness behind him, not wanting his mind proving he was losing it—maybe.

Startled, he came face to face with a solid human. He stumbled backwards, grabbing the kitchen worktop.

'Hello, Owen. I told you I'd see you again,' Abigail mocked him, her hands on her hips. She hoped she looked like she meant business. 'Is your wife home? Wouldn't mind a chat with her.'

'No, she's out, not that it's any business of yours, and how did you get into my house?' he demanded.

'Shouldn't leave your front door wide open. Anyone could walk in.'

Owen stepped toward her. 'You're trespassing.'

'I called out, but no one answered.'

'I see, so you thought you'd just come into my house anyway, Abigail?'

Taken slightly aback that he knew her name, Abigail quickly regained her composure and snorted. 'Yeah, that's me. Lana's best friend.'

She was sure she saw Owen bristle at Lana's name.

'Recognise the name, do you? Lana.'

Owen burst out laughing.

Abigail, annoyed, shouted at him. 'What have you done with Lana?'

Just as quickly as he'd burst out laughing, Owen stopped.

Seeing Owen's weird and angry look, Abigail backed into the hallway, close to the still-open front door.

'I know you were seeing Lana.'

Owen stepped closer to her.

'I've told the police, given them Lana's diary. She's big on writing everything down. About her day, her love.'

Owen looked down at his feet as he took a few steps forward. 'I don't know what you mean. But if what you say is correct, then why aren't the police here instead of you?'

Abigail nervously laughed. 'They're just waiting for the right moment, and they know all I know. Lana is my best friend. We have no secrets.'

The darkness in Owen's eyes had her glancing back at the front door again.

Abigail felt goosebumps up her arms, and the hair on her neck bristled. She sneaked a look at the distance between them. She was glad she'd left the front door wide open.

'You mean HAD no secrets?'

She had to strain her ears to hear his whispered words. What did he say?

With every step he took toward her, Abigail stepped backwards to the door. Still keeping her eyes on him, she said, 'I'm watching you. I know you've got something to do with Lana's disappearance.'

'Watching me?' he scoffed. 'You think I'm involved in your friend's disappearance?'

'I know you are.' Abigail stood her ground. 'I can see it in your eyes. I will get to the bottom of Lana's disappearance, believe me. And I will celebrate when you're locked up in prison for the rest of your life.'

Within four strides, he was at the front door, and anticipating his movement, Abigail ran out of the house.

Owen stood on the threshold and watched Abigail open her car door. She stood half in and half out and stared back at him intently.

'Remember, I'm watching you.'

'And who's watching you, Abigail?' he yelled. 'Oh, by the way, I'll text you.'

Hesitating, she stared back at him. Did he say he'll text me? she thought. She wasn't sure what he said with the wind swirling around. Hurriedly, she got into her car and slammed the door shut.

As she drove away, she glanced in her rearview mirror.

Owen still stood in the doorway, watching her leave. But who was that behind him? She was travelling too fast to make out who it was.

Owen sniggered as he slammed the front door. 'Never had secrets! What a load of shit. If she knew then...well.' he headed back across the hallway to the kitchen when he stopped.

His eyes took in the stairs and the landing. The light coming through the window at the top of the stairs was fading.

He glanced at the front door, convinced it had been sunny outside. Owen put his hand up to his throat. The air felt muggy, claustrophobic even. He tried to gulp to wet his throat as he watched the daylight disappear from the landing window.

In the kitchen, he glanced out of the window and was startled to see the sun still shining at the front of the house.

Owen ran back to the hallway. The sun now glowed through the landing window, and he saw the dust particles dance in the air.

But he stood at the bottom of the stairs, goose bumps on his arms as he took a deep breath. The chill air hurt his lungs, and as he breathed, he could see the cloud of his icy breath.

Owen looked around. There was no one but him. An ice-cold sensation flowed down his arm and into his chest. Struggling to breathe, he turned around.

Nothing.

'Okay, stop it now.' He croaked as his lungs filled with air. 'Don't play with me.'

'No,'

Owen's legs went from under him, and he slammed onto the cold, hard floor. Regaining his breath but stunned, he pushed himself up.

Mid-breath, he stopped and fell back onto the floor. He couldn't move. The crushing on his chest felt like someone was sitting on him, holding him down, holding his arms by his side.

His breath didn't want to leave his lungs.

'Hello.'

Owen's eyes darted from side to side. He tried to get up, but an iciness pounded in his head.

'Hello.'

'Who's there?' he groaned into the shadows he couldn't see.

'Don't forget me, Owen.' 'Get off me,' he rasped.

'Does that feel good, Owen? It didn't to me.'

As quickly as it came, the heaviness in his chest receded. He struggled onto his hands and knees. Without warning, his face smashed into the floor as if someone had grabbed his hair and rammed his face down.

A metallic taste filled his mouth as blood poured out of his mouth and dripped onto the dirty floor.

His stomach churned as the pungent odour engulfed his nostrils. Owen lifted his head and stared at the feet in front of him.

Small, decaying, rotten feet.

With an emerald toe ring on.

'No!' he wailed at the sight in front of him. 'No, not again.' His whole body shook with disbelief at the sight before him.

At the sight of the emerald toe ring, the one he had put on her toe.

Control left him as he felt the warm liquid seep through his trousers and down his legs.

CHAPTER 41

Spud listened as Eric insisted he did. He didn't want to, but Eric's look scared him.

It was the same look his father had when he came back into the house after the incident with his mum.

And from what Eric was saying, it was important for him to listen.

'I'm sorry I didn't tell you this before, Spud, but your father made me promise never to tell you. But seeing as you'll find out eventually, it's best you hear from family. Understood?'

Spud nodded. He'd been waiting a long time to hear the truth, and he didn't want to go off on one when his uncle told him. 'That night your mum left, your dad had something to do with it.'

Spud could feel his anger rising. What the hell was Eric saying? 'My dad made her leave, made my mum leave me behind? No way, Eric. My mum would never have left me behind.'

Eric nervously laughed. 'No, Spud, don't jump to conclusions. That's not what I'm telling you. What I'm telling you is your dad was responsible for your mum leaving.'

'Responsible in what way?.'

'Your dad wasn't proud of his behaviour towards your mum or you. But he was a proud man, and when your mum, in his eyes, defied him and ran from him, he lost it. Ran after her in the rain.'

'I remember. I was watching them from my bedroom window. She ran out, and he ran after her, grabbed her, and led her down the path to the woods.'

Spud's pleading eyes held Eric's. 'Then what happened?'

Tears fell from Eric's red, tired eyes. 'He called me to help him …'

'Help my dad do what?' Spud felt like leaping out of his chair and grabbing at Eric, shaking him, but he needed to stay calm. He desperately wanted Eric to tell him the truth. 'What the hell, Eric?
What did Dad want you to help him with?' his voice raised.

'Calm down, Spud. Listen to me, please. I tried to persuade him to go to the police, but he said no, they'd put him in jail because of all the bruises on her from him beating her.'

'She's dead, isn't she?'

Eric nodded, then stared at the floor

Neither of them said a word for a few minutes.

Finally, Spud looked Eric in the eye. 'Where's my mum, Eric? What did the bastard do to her?'

'I wish I knew. I helped him put your mum in the back seat of my car, but I refused to help him any further. I've no idea where he took her.'

Spud glared at his uncle. 'But I think you do, Eric.'
Spud's fist hit Eric square in the jaw, knocking him flat on the kitchen floor.

'I want the truth. Where is my mum? Where did that bastard take her?' Spud tried to stay calm.

Eric lay on the floor and rubbed his jaw. 'You got some right hook there, Spud.'

Spud grabbed Eric by the shirt collar, almost ripping it, and hauled him to his feet.

'Don't joke with me, Eric. I'm no kid anymore, and I want answers.' Spud pushed him onto the nearest chair. 'Freya Lyle has been helping me. She says there's been some strange things going on in the house. And she found a headstone out the back. Asked me if I wanted to check underneath it.'

'What?' Eric straightened up in the chair. 'You can't do that. You can't dig up a buried coffin without authorisation from the police or someone.'

Spud took a glass from the draining board, filled it from the tap, and took a couple of gulps.

Spud's hand shook with anger, frustration, and hatred for Eric and Seth. He placed the glass back on the draining board.

'Why do you think there's a body under the headstone? Freya said the headstone is on private land, her land. And it looks like it was hidden, on purpose, in the tall grass. Like someone didn't want it found. So, I will ask you, Eric, who are you going to ask? Huh! If no one knows, it's there.'

Eric fidgeted in the chair and felt like screaming at Spud the truth. But he couldn't, not with Spud in such an agitated state.

'Still not right, Spud. You don't know who's buried there, in that spot.'

Spud leaned into Eric, his face so close he could smell the whiskey Eric had been drinking. 'No, Eric, you don't, do ya?'

Eric suddenly shot up, pushing Spud against the sink. The glass rolled off the draining board and smashed into the sink.

'You look here, don't you start insinuating something cos that Mrs Lyle put ideas into your head.'

Picking up a shard of glass, Spud looked at it in the harsh overhead fluorescent light. 'She's been very helpful. Especially since her husband's friend, shall we call her, went missing. Kill two birds with one stone, she said.'

When Spud passed, Eric shrunk away from him and the shard of glass in his hand. Spud looked Eric straight in the eye. 'She told me there had been a lot of strange things going on in the house. What is strange is that her dog won't go into the woods to do his business or play. He'd go straight around the back.'

'Maybe it's too dark for him.' Eric mumbled.

'Okay, I'll give you time, Eric, but I know you're hiding something from me. I'll not wait much longer. I want the truth from you. Understand?'

Eric nodded.

Left in the kitchen, Eric picked up the shards of glass from the sink.

In the garden, he threw the shards of glass into the bin.

The light from Spud's bedroom illuminated the garden, creating a dull, eery glow around him. The chill air made its presence felt. 'Shit', he said under his breath.

In the past, he had managed to make the life of any occupant of Blyneath hell.

He would bury carcasses in and around the grounds, rotting and smelling like a slaughterhouse.

His favourite thing to do was make strange noises in the night. He knew every nook and cranny in the house and could set up creaks and groans anywhere.

But that all changed when the Lyle's moved in.

Things were happening that had nothing to do with him.

What? He didn't know.

But the one thing he did know, Owen Lyle was the cause of it all.

CHAPTER 42

The outstretched hand tried to grab him, but couldn't reach him. He had to get away, had to run, run, run. Had to run from the noise, from the damn tapping noise. He jumped out of bed, brushing away at the hands on his arms.

'Freya!'.

Jolted out of sleep by the shout of her name, Freya scrambled for the sidelight. 'What are you doing?'

Owen desperately clawed at the bedroom door handle, trying to open it. She quickly got to him, grabbed his hands from the door handle, and tried to shake him.

'Owen, wake up.' She screamed in his face. 'Stop this now.'

Owen tried to push her away, but she grabbed his top and, in his frightened, fragile state, easily threw him onto the floor.

'Didn't you hear it?' he babbled as he stared at the door. 'I heard something.'

Freya grabbed his face. 'I don't give a shit what you THINK you heard, what you THINK you bloody saw. Get your arse off the floor and get back in bed. I'm sick of this, all of this.'

She ignored his attempts to get up and left him floundering on the floor like a seal.

'No,' he wailed. 'Don't go out there.' He stared after Freya as she stormed out of the bedroom.

'There's no one out here, you idiot.' Freya slammed the door behind her.

Owen crawled to the door, cracked it open, and peeked out onto the landing. Slowly, he got to his feet, and step by step, he left the bedroom.

'There it is.' He said to the gloom around him. 'Tap! Tap!

Tap!' His hand tapped on the handrail.

'Owen?' Freya came up the stairs with a glass of water.

'I can hear it.' Owen whispered.

At the top of the stairs, Freya rolled her eyes. 'No. There is no noise coming from anywhere in this house except you.'

'Who's there?' he asked. 'Is that you again?'

Freya got to him just in time before he threw himself down the stairs.

CHAPTER 43

Freya couldn't take anymore, and once she had settled Owen back in bed, she decided to call Abigail. After a dozen rings, Abigail finally answered the phone. 'Hello,' she sounded drowsy.

'I'm sorry it's so early, Abigail, but he's had another nightmare. This time, he tried to throw himself down the stairs. I can't take any more of this.'

Should have let him, Abigail thought. But said. 'About Lana again?'

Freya turned the corner of the house and shone her torch towards the headstone. 'I don't know anymore. Earlier, he was convinced a tapping noise was coming from the landing. All he could say was, is that you again? So who freaking knows? I need to confront him. About his affair with Lana.'

'Where is Owen now?'

'A sleep. I'm standing in the back garden, and it's so dark and, if I'm being honest, I'm scared.'

'Of what? Owen?'

'No, of this place, and what is going on because something bloody well is?'

Freya could hear Abigail click the kettle on. 'And whatever is going on, it's after Owen. He's the one who's seeing things and hearing things.' Freya had purposely not mentioned the voice in her head, pleading with her to help her to Abigail.

Freya thought she could have helped as she talked to Abigail by letting him fall down the stairs. But she couldn't let Owen get away with what he'd done so easily. 'Although I think he tried to convince me once that I was having a nightmare. Something was pulling me to the unused room down the landing. And now I think about it, Owen doesn't like that room. Says it gives him the creeps.' Freya paused. 'And whatever it is, whatever is happening, it's getting in his head.

He's getting worse and his moods are swinging high, low, to downright aggressive. After what you told me, Abigail, what my husband is capable of ...' Freya couldn't bring herself to finish the sentence. 'What if he turns on me? He obviously doesn't know that I know.'

Abigail sighed. 'I know I've put you in an impossible situation. But, Freya, I'm so grateful that you believe me.'

Unexpectedly, Freya let out a sob. 'It hurts so much after everything I've been through. For him to play around while I'm going through shit.'

'I'm so sorry, Freya.'

Freya took a deep breath. 'No, there's no need to be, Abigail. But I can't go on like this. I bet you he'll have another nightmare. And this time? Who knows what he will do? I need to confront him. Ask him what the hell is going on.'

'Just be careful, Freya, and if you need help, please ask me.'

Freya walked back around the front of the house, her feet crunching on the driveway. 'I will. I'll speak to you soon. Oh, and Abigail? Leave Owen to me. I don't want you getting hurt.'

'I'll try, but I'm not going to promise.'

CHAPTER 44

Owen pulled up in front of his house and laboriously got out of the car.

He knew he shouldn't have gone to work this morning after the incident last night. Owen recalled the anger on Freya's face as he, again, screamed about hearing tapping noises.

He knew he had, and Freya's quick action stopped him from jumping off the landing and down the stairs. She could have easily let him fall. Freya was so angry with him that she'd ignored him this morning.

He couldn't concentrate on anything, and the thought of that lout Nathan snooping through the woods had him panicked.

Voices coming from the back of the house caught his attention. Unsure of what to expect, he cautiously made his way to the back of the house, where the sight of Freya and Nathan, deep in conversation, greeted him.

'Well, this looks cosy.' He scorned.

'Oh, Owen, you're home early.' Freya headed toward him and went to kiss him on the cheek, but Owen turned away from her.

'Owen, what's the matter?'

Owen stepped toward Nathan, who, seeing the snarl of his mouth and the irrational look in his eyes, stepped back.

'Look, I don't know what your problem is with me.'

'Why would I have a problem with the handyman? Umm, tell me, I'd really like to know.' Owen took a few more steps toward Nathan, who, this time, stood his ground.

Seeing Owen's clenched fists, Freya grabbed his arm to pull him back. 'Owen, what the hell are you doing?'

Owen turned on her. 'Like little chit-chat with your lover boy, do you?'

'What? Stop, Owen.' She pulled hard on his arm this time, forcing him to step backwards.

'Nothing is going on with Nathan and me, you stupid idiot.' She fired a quick look at Nathan.

'Maybe I should leave.' Nathan headed out of Owen's way back to the front of the house.

Freya watched Nathan leave, and once he was out of sight, slapped Owen across the face. 'How dare you?' she spat. 'How dare you accuse Nathan and me of doing something we shouldn't?'

Freya could feel the blood rush to her face. She didn't care she had just lied straight to Owen's face. He didn't deserve any truth from her, except she was going to leave him.

But she would tell Owen in good time. In her own time.

Owen stood there, shocked by Freya's anger. 'I'm sorry. It's been stressful at work lately.'

'Another lame excuse.' As Freya stormed back to the house, she turned to look at her dishevelled, broken-looking husband. 'You're walking on thin ice, Owen. I suggest that whatever is going on with you, you'd better sort it out. I can't deal with this anymore.' Freya put her hands on her hips. 'And I'm not going to.'

Everything around him seemed to blur. He stood rooted to the spot, blinking rapidly, trying to restore his vision in time to see Freya turn the corner of the house.

He was losing her. A shudder overtook him, and he could feel tears stinging his eyes. What the hell was he doing? Why didn't he pack up and leave and go back to the city where he and Freya belonged, not out here, in this shithole?

Why didn't they just up and leave? He knew exactly why.

A cool autumn breeze ruffled his hair. The swishing noise of the trees as they swayed in the breeze filled his head.

Owen closed his eyes. He could smell the clear air and he filled his lungs as much as he could. He closed his eyes to the sun.

Unexpectedly, he felt a hand on his shoulder, and he smiled.

'Freya, I knew you couldn't be mad at me for long.' Her hand gripped harder on his shoulder. 'Come on, Freya, hold my hand.'

He felt her hand glide down his arm and slide into his hand.

'Wow, your hand is freezing.' He turned to hug Freya to warm her up.

No one was there. No one held his hand. He staggered backwards.

Suddenly, his legs gave way, and he fell hard on the grass. He clutched at his chest. His heart felt like an iron fist had grabbed his heart and squeezed it hard.

A face loomed over him and he reached up to touch it, but it moved out of reach.

'Freya.' He mouthed, 'Don't leave me.'

The face came closer. The lank blond hair dangled in his face, and the dull blue eyes bore into his.

'It's me'

Terrified screams had Freya running towards her husband, who lay on the ground clutching his chest and with a wild, terrified look in his eyes.

CHAPTER 45

The doctor stood over Owen, clipboard in hand, and looked at the clipboard again before placing it back at the bottom of the hospital bed.

'You've been lucky, Mr Lyle. It wasn't a heart attack, more like a panic attack. Maybe your body's telling you to slow down. High blood pressure isn't good for you. Are you stressed at work?' Owen slowly nodded.

'He told me he was stressed at work. But I didn't think it was this bad.'

Freya touched the doctor's arm, 'He's been having terrible nightmares, so bad he wakes up screaming. A scream I've never heard from him… or anyone else before.'

The doctor nodded. 'Okay. After a few more days in the hospital, I suggest a few days off at home to relax and build your strength up. I'll sort out your release from the hospital, Mr Owen, and I want you to take my advice. You're not getting any younger, and, god forbid, the next chest pains could be it.'

Freya waited for the doctor to leave the room before she leaned into her husband and hissed. 'You and I need to have a serious talk when you get out of hospital.'

'I know, I know. I've got to stop stressing and being insulting. Isn't that what you said? Just before I collapsed with a heart attack?'

Fuming, Freya moved closer to Owen's ear. 'Don't you dare? What I heard you say when I ran to you, when I heard you scream, I wish you had had a heart attack.'

She paused and stared at the puzzled look on her husband's face. 'Don't remember that bit, do you? Would you like me to remind you?'

Anxiously, Owen shook his head. Before he passed out on the grass, he remembered seeing a face he knew leaning over him, with blond hair and blue eyes. There was no way he was going to tell Freya that.

'Whatever I said, I didn't mean it; I was in distress, thinking I was having a heart attack.'

Freya continued, regardless. 'I quote "Lana. I'm sorry for what I've done." Unquote. What the hell did you mean by that? Isn't Lana the name of the missing woman from the newspaper? The one you told me you didn't know. The one you told me you'd never met?'

'I told you, Freya, I don't know her. All I know about her is what I've read in the paper.' Owen felt the room spin and squeezed shut his eyes. This couldn't be happening to him.

'Don't shut your eyes on me. You're a liar, Owen Lyle. I know you knew her. Knew her a lot. I want to hear the truth from your mouth.'

His mind rushed with the thought he had to leave the hospital. There was no way he was going to stay a minute longer. He would have to discharge himself ASAP.

He had to get back and check the woods. Again. Check the spot where he'd ... surely the hole was deep enough.

Owen suddenly felt queasy. 'I need to rest, ' he said, putting his hand up to his forehead. 'My head is hurting big time,' he added.

'I bet it is.' Freya mocked into his face. 'I can't stand to be near you, ' she said, picking up her bag.

As she was leaving, she said, 'Oh, and don't think I'll be visiting you anytime soon.'

He watched her leave and then breathed a sigh of relief. He felt tired, and his head really did hurt.

Owen closed his eyes, desperate for sleep, before he made his move to leave. But sleep wouldn't take him. Instead, the time he wished he could have over again engulfed his brain.

CHAPTER 46

Owen squeezed her knee as the car bumped along the dirt track and up to a peeling, rotten, lopsided wooden fence.

'Wow! Owen, this looks amazing! All these trees.' The woman squealed with delight.

Owen laughed. 'You are so easily pleased. This is just the beginning of the land surrounding the house. Another few minutes, and we'll be there.'

As he stopped the car, he turned to the woman. 'Close the gate once I'm through, will you?'

She jumped out and did as she was told, straining to lift the gate and drag it to one side.

As they got closer to the house, along the dirt track, Owen put his arm around the woman and pulled her closer to him. 'Close your eyes, Lana.' She put her hands over her eyes, too, for good measure.

The car slowed, and Owen removed his arm from her shoulders and brushed a loose strand of her blond hair from her face.

'Open your eyes.'

Lana opened her eyes a bit at a time, not sure what to expect.

'Wow.' She marvelled at the house in front of her. 'It…it… looks.'

'Fabulous?' Owen laughed.

'No, it looks old.' Lana scrunched up her nose as she got out of the car.

She gazed at the bay window on the right side of the house and a large window to her left. Both looked cloudy from years of dust and grime.

Owen stood beside her and put his arm around her waist. She gently pulled away from him and headed for the front door.

'I'd change this colour to dark blue.' Lana announced as her fingers traced the faded lime green paint.

She turned to Owen, who still stood by the side of his car, and smiled. 'It'll suit the place better.'

Owen pulled a key from his jacket pocket and jiggled it playfully as he joined her at the front door. 'Let's go inside.'

The sunlight broke into the hallway as the front door creaked open on rusted hinges. Lana followed Owen into the gloomy hallway; their footsteps echoed around them. Owen began to close the door.

'No, leave it open, Owen, please. It's dark in here, and I don't like it.'

He left the door wide open. 'There's nothing to be afraid of. It's just an old house.'

Lana held tightly onto his arm. 'That's why I don't like it. It's an old house, and you know what comes with an old house. Ghosts.'

Owen's laugh startled her as it echoed around the hallway, bouncing off the walls and high ceiling.

'Don't laugh. I'm serious.'

'Come on, let's go this way.'

Their feet left footprints on the dusty wooden floor as they came to what had once been a kitchen.

195

'Blimey.' Lana looked around the kitchen, which had broken cabinets and cracked tiled floors. The sink had patches of rust in its aluminium bottom, and what looked like rat droppings littered the sink and along the worktops. 'That is disgusting.'

She stepped away from the sink and headed back into the hallway.

'What's the matter? Don't you like it?' Owen's harsh tone made Lana stop in her tracks.

She turned to him. 'Do I like it? Why would I like it, Owen? I'm not going to live here.' she studied his face. 'Am I?

Owen crossed the kitchen floor in four strides and put his arms around her waist. 'I know it looks like a dump, but it's only on the surface. The walls are solid. There's plenty of land. And the woods.' He let go of her and stood in front of the kitchen window above the sink, spreading his arms wide. 'Comes with the property.'

A sudden bang from the top of the house startled Lana. 'What the hell was that?' she clung to Owen's arm.

'It was probably the wind.' He tugged Lana's hands off him. 'Come on, let's go upstairs, check where the bang came from.'

'Are you crazy? What did I say about old houses and ghosts?'

Owen turned to her. 'There is no such thing as ghosts. Now stop being so stupid. Come on, upstairs.'

She saw the annoyance on his face and, without another word, followed him toward the staircase.

The creak of the stairs did nothing for Lana's nerves as she tried to calm herself. She held onto the wooden handrail and repeatedly looked behind her. 'I don't like this,' she said.

Owen stopped near the top of the stairs and looked back down at her. 'If you don't like it, we'll leave.' Without waiting for her to answer, he continued onto the landing.

At the top of the stairs, he waited for her to join him.

'Now, I'm thinking, this room.' he headed to the door on the left of the landing, and Lana quietly followed him.

He pushed open the door, and it gently hit the wall. 'Will be the bedroom.'

Lana approached cautiously. She felt uneasy and kept looking behind her down the landing to the end, where a door was closed. Had it been that door that banged?

Owen stood there, framed in the doorway. What sunlight that could get through the dirty windows cast a shadow across his face.

Lana wasn't sure what his face was telling her. Was he angry at her for being scared, or was he frustrated at her lack of enthusiasm about the house?

After all, wasn't Owen going to buy this house for her?

In her head, she told herself off for being stupid. It was just an old house, as Owen had said. Old houses have creaks. She forced herself to smile.

Owen looked out the bedroom's front window. Woods surrounded the house on three sides, and a dirt track snaked through the trees, ending in front of the house.

A heady scent of pine and after-rain dampness filled the air.

'*Watch out.*'

'What was that?' Lana spun around in the doorway and stared at the dimly lit landing. Wasn't the door at the far end closed before? she thought, her head cocked, trying to listen for noises.

Something spooked her. Lana wasn't a person who imagined things, at least not until now. Why did the door at the end of the landing creep her out? She'd never been here before.

'*Watch out.*'

'Owen, did you hear that?' she whimpered. When he didn't answer, she went back into the bedroom. Owen looked deep in thought as he gazed out of the back bedroom window, which looked out onto an overgrown garden. 'Owen, did you hear that?' Lana came up behind him and put her arm around his waist. She felt comfort knowing he was here.

'What's so interesting out there?'

'Nothing.' He removed her arms around his waist.

Lana felt lost. She didn't know how to react to Owen's mood; she had never seen him like this.

'Why are you thinking about buying this house, Owen? It's nothing like your fantastic apartment in the city.'

Owen pondered the question, his gaze transfixed on the ground below. 'I don't know.' he turned to face her. 'I know my apartment in the city is fantastic, with fabulous views of the park and the lower city. But.' He exhaled. 'I think a change of scene will do me good. Anyway, I need a project. Something to keep my mind off my problems.' He strode past her, back onto the landing.

'Problems?' Lana hesitated, then followed him downstairs.

'Aren't you going to see the rest of the house?' Her voice echoed. The light from the landing window at the top of the stairs hardly reached the hallway, and the long shadows only enhanced Lana's uncomfortable feelings about the house.

Owen shook his head and paused as he took in the dusty hallway and the dim light from the landing window. He glanced toward the kitchen to his left, then to his right, where double wooden doors were closed.

'I suppose I should.' He frowned and headed for the closed doors.

They creaked open. It was just another empty, dusty, grimy room with a bay window overlooking the driveway and another overlooking the overgrown back garden. It had a small fireplace on the back wall, to Owen's delight.

'Owen, can I ask you a question?'

Owen turned to her. 'Of course.'

She cleared her throat. 'Why have you brought me here? Are you going to buy this house for us?'

Ignoring her question, he went back to the hallway. Lana followed him and waited patiently for his answer as he stood, hands in pockets, looking around again.

'You know what? I hadn't really decided, and even though I knew I wanted it, I couldn't give myself a good enough reason to buy it. But I think I will. This house needs new life breathed into it. The potential is enormous,'

Lana suddenly grabbed him and clamped her arms around him. 'You really think we can make it our home?' her voice sounded muffled against his chest, but Owen had heard her clearly.

Lana felt his body stiffen. 'Owen, what's the matter?' She looked up at him.

He turned to face her. 'I think we need to talk.'

Lana's heart raced as she stared into his serious face. 'Oh.'

Without saying a word, he went outside and leaned against his car.

'What is it?' she stood in front of her lover, her voice a slight tremor. He was the only man she had ever loved so deeply that it hurt and the only man she had ever made love to. 'What do you need to talk about?'

She couldn't keep a smile from forming at the corner of her mouth. Was this the moment he was going to propose? She hoped so.

The timing couldn't be better.

Owen hesitated before he answered. 'I can't do this anymore, Lana. I don't know what the hell I've been doing. Stupid, stupid. I've...I've something to tell you.'

Lana's smile instantly disappeared. She felt she was going to faint, and not wanting to show herself up in front of Owen, she leaned against the bonnet of the car. 'What can't you do anymore, Owen? Tell me because right now I feel very confused.'

His eyes bore into hers. 'I thought I'd buy this house, no matter what.'

'No matter what?' Lana tucked a loose bit of her blond hair behind her ear.

'To get away from the city. To get away from...' He stormed back into the house.

Surprised when he headed back to the house, Lana could only hurry after him. 'To get away from the city?' she was so confused by this side of Owen, by all the sides of him he was showing her today. His sharp tone, his annoyance with her. She'd never seen him like this before, and she didn't like it.

Back inside the house, in the hallway, Owen turned to her. 'You and me, Lana. We've had a good time, haven't we?'

Lana apprehensively nodded as panic rose into her chest. She would not let this happen, and she had a bad feeling about what Owen was going to say to her. She had to change his mind.

'No, wait. I have some news for you.' She took hold of his hands, squeezed them hard, and looked up at him.

She forced a smile.

Owen stood straight. 'What?'

Lana's smile softened and became more natural. She let go of his hands and stroked his chest.

'I'm pregnant.... and we can live in this house, together, as a family.'

Owen saw the look of hope in her eyes.

In his, she saw horror.

'You're pregnant?'

'Yes, that happens when we have unprotected sex.'

He shoved past her. 'You're pregnant?' He turned to her. His face was hard as he slapped his head. 'How stupid can you get?'

Lana, her heart racing and her hands trembling, forced a smile. His reaction nerved her. 'Isn't it great?' she involuntarily giggled and held out her hand to Owen, hoping he would take it and hug her tight, tell her everything would be okay.

But Owen turned on her. 'Are you fucking stupid? Do you think it's funny?' He snapped.

'Owen!'

He stormed out of the house and around to the back, his jacket flapping behind him in his rush to get away from her. His shoulders drooped. 'I don't believe this.'

He heard her run after him. Her heels crunched on the loose stones.

'I thought this was why you brought me here.' Lana gasped.

'To show me how much you love me, that you wanted to marry me, and we could make the house a home, our home.'

'What the hell made you think I was going to buy this house for us?'

Startled, Lana stopped in her tracks. 'Owen, you said it would make a great home. You talked about the bedroom and how the woods came with the house. I thought you were thinking about me and you, here, starting a family.'

He turned his back on her and stared into the woods ahead of him. 'How far gone are you?'

Lana stood behind him. Tears pricked her eyes, and she tried not to sniffle.

Owen heard her sniffle and tried to resist the urge to turn around and see the woman he had been having an affair with standing there looking weak. Thinking he could upset her like this, make her beg for him to stay with her, made him smile. He couldn't understand why. Why upsetting another person would give him such satisfaction.

But at the end of the day, he thought, this is what he did. This is my job: to upset people and put them in their place.

'Three months.'

Owen whirled around. 'Three months!'

Behind Owen, a rustling sound came from the woods.

He squinted into the trees. 'Who's there?' he shouted.

The trees shifted in front of him. He was certain he could see someone hiding in the trees. 'If you don't come out, I'm coming in, and god help whoever is there.'

'Don't you think that's strange?' Lana wiped at her eyes.

'What's fucking strange, Lana, that you wait until now to tell me you're three months pregnant?'

She gulped to keep the tears at bay. 'No, that the trees there behind you are moving like there is some wind while the others are still. And I can't feel any breeze.' she raised her palm.

Irritated, Owen turned his attention back to the trees. Lana was right. Only a few trees were moving.

'Is there anyone there? Come out.' There was another rustling noise, and Owen stepped forward.

Lana squeezed his arm. 'Come on, Owen, let's go.'

He shrugged her off and headed back to the house. 'We have to talk about this.'

Franticly, she followed him, but something made her give the woods one more glance.

Abruptly, she stopped and took a step toward the swaying trees. Was there someone watching her?

'Hello.' She called out, convinced there was someone there. 'I can see you.' Someone was staring at her. She squeezed her eyes against the lowering rays of the late afternoon sun.

Was that a woman she could see staring back at her? Lana approached the figure hiding behind a tree trunk.

She could just make out her face in the shadows and her long, dark hair. The woman seemed to put a finger to her lips as if to quiet Lana.

'Hello.' Lana whispered. 'Who are you?'

'Lana!' Owen barked for her to get to him.

'Sorry, I have to go.' Lana stared as the woman came from behind the tree.

'*No, don't.*'

'Lana.' Owen's angry shout reverberated around the woods.

'He's angry. I have to go.'

Owen and Lana sat at an old table left in the kitchen. A couple of broken chairs lay against a cupboard, but two were okay to sit on.

'What do you expect of me?' Owen demanded, tapping his fingers impatiently on the table. 'What do you think is going to happen between us?'

'I know you love me, Owen. You have no commitments, you have a good job. I bless the day Alan Unsworth took me on, saying I had potential.'

He held his head. 'I can't believe this.' He avoided looking at her. 'I was going to end our relationship because…'

'Because of what, Owen? Because you're so much older than me. I don't care. I love you. I love your grey hair, how you take care of yourself, how smart you are and how you treat me like a princess.'

She smiled coyly. 'I especially love how you fuck me.' she could feel a redness spreading across her chest and up into her cheeks. She never used such coarse language.

It panicked Lana that Owen seemed unmoved by her frank statement.

Owen picked at his nails. 'Because my wife is getting suspicious,' he said. 'There, it's out in the open. Thank the Lord. It's been tough keeping the fact I'm married to an amazing woman from you.' He chuckled.

Owen's confession hung in the air as Lana's fraught eyes stared in disbelief.

'You're married?' her voice was barely a whisper. 'And I'm carrying your child.' She stood so quickly her chair fell over. 'You … you bastard. You told me you were a widower. How sick is that to tell me your wife was dead? And now you tell me how amazing she is? How could you deliberately lie to me?' Lana couldn't believe how calm she felt, how composed in the light of her lover's confession.

Owen kicked his chair away and banged his fist on the dining table.

Before she knew it, he was in her face. She felt his hot breath and could sense he was just about keeping calm. Her calmness and composure soon disappeared.

'I have a wife. I'm sorry I led you to the wrong conclusion about me.'

'Wrong conclusion. There wasn't any wrong conclusion. You lied to me.'

Owen straightened and shrugged his shoulders. 'Yes, I guess that's the truth.'

As soon as he stood away from her, Lana ran into the hallway, desperately wanting a safe distance between them. 'So, what happens now, Owen? I'm carrying your baby. What will your amazing wife think of that?'

Panic rose in her as she saw his face contort into hate. His eyes were full of rage as he stormed toward her.

Terrified, Lana backed away. The front door was closed, and panicked, she ran up the stairs. At the top of the stairs, Lana stopped, breathing rapidly, her hands clamped on the handrail.

Owen, at the bottom of the stairs, looked up at Lana, the frightened girl he had lured into bed. 'I'm sorry,' he said as he climbed the stairs slowly, deliberately, keeping his eyes on Lana.

Lana staggered back against the wall. 'Please, Owen, stop.' In her panic, she ran for the nearest door.

The door was stiff, and as fear took hold of her at Owen's footsteps coming up the stairs, she desperately shoved with all her might.

The hinges squeaked as the door flung open, and it smashed against the wall, the crash reverberated around the room.

Lana grabbed the door to slam it shut against the advancing Owen.

But Owen was too quick for her. Before she could close the door, he was through it, and he grabbed her arms and forced her into the centre of the room. 'No one tells Owen Lyle to stop.' He pressed her against the window.

The glass was cold against her back, and she could feel the give of the glass.

'An accident could happen right here,' he taunted into her face.

'Please, Owen. The baby.'

'Please, Owen, the baby,' he imitated her. 'Just one little push against this window and, well, it'll be goodbye Lana … and your baby.'

The window cracked, and Lana could feel the cold outside on her back.

'Please.' she cried.

He flung her onto the dusty, grimy wooden floor. She lay there, not daring to move. Tears came hard and fast as she trembled.

'Owen.' She pleaded.

He straddled her. 'Shall we have a fuck before we leave?'

'What?' Lana's head couldn't understand what Owen had just said. Was he being nice and kind to her again, or was he being hurtful?

'Come on, like you said, you liked how I fuck you.'

Owen put his hand up her dress and began to pull her underwear down.

'Stop.' Lana screamed at the top of her voice. 'Please, Owen, stop.'

Owen got off her and knelt beside her. Then, gently, he brushed her hair from her face and stroked it.

Lana recoiled at his touch but kept her eyes on his face. 'What are you doing?'

'I'm so sorry, Lana. I'm so sorry.' He stood. 'Come on.' he held his hand out to help her to her feet.

'You scared me, Owen.' Reluctantly, she took his hand.

He hugged her tightly. 'I'm sorry.'

She felt the breath in her expel in tearful bursts.

Owen stroked her back as he held her in his arms. Suddenly, his hands were on her throat, his big, strong hands squeezing and squeezing.

She tried to take a gulp of air as blackness came toward her.

With all her strength, she kicked Owen in between his legs, and he went down in a heap.

'Bitch.' Owen curled up on the floor, holding himself, and Lana, hurting for breath, staggered from the room.

The stairs seemed a long way away, but she would not die here, not at the hands of the man she loved. Her only thought was the life she was carrying. Her heart raced as she staggered to the top of the stairs.

She grabbed the handrail with one hand and, taking a deep breath, began to descend to the hallway and, she hoped, take Owen's car and get away from him, get away from the man she thought she knew.

'Lana.' Owen's pained voice halted her. 'Please, I'm sorry, so, so, sorry.'

She heard him sob. 'Please, forgive me. I didn't mean to hurt you.'

He was on his hands and knees, his hands in prayer. 'Please.'

Lana, a foot on the top stair, hesitated. She stared at Owen as he got to his feet and made his way along the landing towards her.

'I love you.' He reached for her and touched her arm. 'Please.'

Her whole being screamed at her to run, run as fast as she could away from this man and this house.

But he loves me, she thought, and I'm going to have his baby.'

Owen took her arm and walked at her side, gently guiding her down the stairs and out into the sunshine.

Confused, Lana blinked into the semi-blue sky and looked back toward the house.

She was sure the sun had gone behind the trees. Wasn't the light fading in the hallway earlier? She shook the thought from her head.

Lana leaned against the car, her hand on her stomach. 'I don't like this, this part of you. You can't behave like you wanted to kill me one minute and then be kind the next.' She paused. What was she thinking? Did she really want to be with a man who put his hands on her and cheated on his wife?

His wife. The word stuck in her throat.

She opened the car door. 'I think your wife needs to know what kind of nasty, crazed, cheat of a husband you are.'

Before she could get into the car, Lana felt hands on her shoulders.

Owen spun her round to face him. 'No one threatens me.'

'I'm not threatening you, Owen.' She stepped away from him, keeping a distance between them. 'You lied to me, had me believing you were free to marry me.'

Owen smirked. 'Oh, Lana, dear Lana. What makes you think I would want to marry you, even if I was free?'

'You bastard. I'm leaving.' Lana headed unsteadily down the driveway. Not looking where she was going, she stumbled over a rock and onto her knees.

Owen was with her in an instant, helping her to her feet. 'I'll take you home.'

She let him help her back to the car, but he stopped and instead of helping her into the car, said. 'Lana, let me take a photo of you.'

'What? Are you joking? No, you need to take me home. Now.'

Owen grabbed her by the arms and forced her to the front of the car. 'Come on, for old times' sake, just for me, ' he said, looking deeply into Lana's eyes, his lips inches from hers.

'I… I don't know.' She felt helpless under his gaze, and when his lips brushed hers, she knew he had her right where he wanted her.

And there was nothing she could do about it.

'Okay.' She breathed.

'My phone is in the car; I'll just get it.' Owen jumped into the car, turned the engine on, and, hands shaking, quickly turned it off again because, for a split second, he considered driving over Lana.

'Why did you turn the engine on, Owen?' Lana held up a hand to shield her eyes from the sun.

'Just checking my phone charge.'

Owen loomed over her and rubbed her arms, then her shoulders. His fingers stroked the back of her neck.

'What are you doing?' Lana said.

'Just keeping you warm. It's getting chilli now.'

She shoved his hands off her. 'Your hand was on my neck again.'

Owen put his hands up. 'I'm sorry. I'd never hurt you. But you must understand things between us have changed.'

'You'd never hurt me? What the hell just happened in that room?' she pointed at the last room on the top floor. Even from here, she could see the crack in the windowpane. 'You tried to push me out of the window and then strangle me? You're the one who changed things.' Lana suddenly felt some courage. She stood her ground. 'I'm going to keep this baby, our baby. So, Mr big shot, Mr adulterer, you can go to hell.'

She headed back down the dirt track. 'I want to go home. I'll make my own way back. You stay away from me.'

Owen waited a few seconds, then ran after her. 'Lana, Lana, I was joking.' He stepped in front of her. 'I'm just shocked by the news and panicked. I'm not married. Honest.'

His stifled laughter told her otherwise.

'I don't believe you,' she continued down the track. How can she trust a person who tried to strangle her?

After several more steps, she saw the rock she'd stumbled over. Then she gazed at the long track ahead of her through the woods.

She didn't want to walk alone. Lana glanced up at the darkening sky and was sure she felt drops of rain.

She spun around. 'I've changed my mind. You can take me home.'

He spun her around and pointed at the run-down house before them. 'Look, this can be our home. You can even have the kitchen of your dreams. I promise I'll look after you.'

Suddenly, Owen was down on one knee and took Lana's hands in his. 'Will you marry me?'

Shocked, Lana tried to pull her hands free. 'No. You're a married man, Owen, and I don't believe you anymore, and I think your poor wife should know what kind of husband she has.'

Owen bowed his head. 'Okay. But help me up, will you?'

Lana, irritated, helped him up. He grunted as he straightened up.

They stared at each other.

In a flash, Owen grabbed her by the throat and staggered her backwards as he stood up to his full height.

He threw her to the ground, and as he leaned over her, she tried to scream.

'You can scream all you want. There's no one here to hear you.'

In his desire to stop Lana, at any cost, from ruining his marriage, he never noticed the figure in the woods, watching him commit murder.

CHAPTER 47

Owen struggled to get out of the taxi. Refusing to listen to the Doctor, he discharged himself from the hospital. And now he wished he had listened as, in his weak state, the high winds threatened to pull the taxi door from him.

The outside lights came on, and Owen was relieved he'd relented when Freya told him Nathan had thought it a good idea to have security lights out in front of the house.

He steadied himself in the wind as he watched the taxi disappear into the darkness. Owen staggered toward the front door, trying to pick the front door key from all the others he had on his car keys. He was glad he'd insisted he and Freya had their own set of keys. His hands shook as he tried to pick the right key to unlock the front door.

Finally, he was in and pushed open the front door. He stepped inside and switched on the hall lights.

Owen moved through the house and switched all the lights on. He felt a need to have light around him. The darkness had the potential to hurt him, and he wasn't taking any chances.

In his haste to light the house, he forgot he had left the front door wide open.

'What shall we do, Rose?'

'Let him settle in first, then we'll go pay him a visit.'

Owen staggered into the kitchen and grabbed a bottle of beer from the fridge and screwed off the top, and downed the beer in one go.

Straight away, he felt his head spin. He shouldn't have downed the beer so fast, not just coming out of the hospital, but he didn't care.

He looked around the kitchen at the scrubbed floor and the fixed cupboards. 'Damn piece of shit.' He muttered. 'Like everything else in this crap place.'

He didn't like the house anymore.

In fact, he never did. It was just a means to an end. A means for him to hide his mess in the woods.

It was his property; he would severely deal with anyone who strayed onto it.

Slowly, Owen climbed the stairs, holding on to the wooden handrail for support. As he approached the top, his eyes darted left to right, as if waiting for someone or something to jump out at him. Finally, on the landing, he switched the lamp on and looked out of the window into the darkness of the back garden below.

Nothing.

The drugs the doctor had prescribed him were in his trouser pocket. He took them out and stared at them. 'I could take them all, and that would be the end of my troubles, my nightmares.'

'Would it?'

'What...who's there?' he spun around so fast his eyes seemed to bounce from side to side against his skull as he tried to focus around him.

He listened. Then he noticed the open front door. A mist swirled leaves across the hallway, and a bone-chilling coldness hit him.

'Shit. Don't be so stupid.' He uttered out loud. The echo of his voice unnerved him in the house's quiet.

He felt an impulse, a pull to the door at the end of the landing, the one where… No, he would not think about that. 'Shit. Nothing in that room.' But he felt he had no say in where his legs took him. He swayed toward the room, steadying himself with a hand on the wall.

Had to have a look.

Now, the door was in front of him. 'Looks harmless enough.' He thought more to convince himself.

He reached out a hand to turn the handle, but he stopped when he heard a knock behind him. 'What was that?' he looked back at the top of the stairs again.

His head hurt and his eyes blurred in the dim light. He blinked to clear his vision.

'Owen, stop scaring yourself.' He turned his attention back to the door and gently wrapped his hand around the handle.

Abruptly, he pulled his hand away. 'Bloody hell, that's cold.' Owen shook his hand to get the blood flowing and tried again.

He gripped the handle and yanked it down, but didn't open the door.

He let his hand linger there for a second, even though the cold of the handle hurt.

'Stupid idea.' He stood looking at his hand on the door handle for a few seconds, then decided to open the door.

It gently swung open a couple of feet.

He didn't know what to expect. A chilling creak of the door hinges? Someone behind the door ready to jump out at him? But the door didn't creak, and there was no one behind the door.

Owen gingerly poked his head into the room, then his body, and before he knew it, he stood in the middle of an empty room.

Alone.

There was no carpet or furniture, only the faint smell of paint lingering from Nathan's window frame repair, and Owen felt relieved that the cracked window had been replaced.

But it was so cold.

He looked out of the window, down at the driveway, and into the darkness. The taxi driver remarked why anyone would want to live out here. He had a point.

Owen couldn't help himself. His eyes rested on the woods— the dark, foreboding woods with trees that swayed in the wind. There was always wind, always the trees swayed in the bloody wind, he thought.

Owen pressed his nose against the glass pane and squinted at the moonlight that looked to dance between the trees, where their trunks were like legs in a cabaret show.

Startled, he banged his head on the window.

Legs!

Did he just see legs? He scanned the nearest tree trunks, the cabaret show.

'Bloody hell, I shouldn't have had beer on top of my medication. Now I'm seeing tree trunks with human legs.'

He turned around and leaned against the window to look around the empty room.

The room that scared him.

For good reason.

Then his eyes settled on the door.

The closed door.

Owen rubbed his eyes, contemplating whether he had closed the door. He shoved off the window. Gingerly, he curled his fingers around the handle. It still felt cold.

Owen wanted to throw the door open and run down the landing, run down the stairs, run away, far away from his nightmares, far away from this cursed house.

But he was so tired.

He let the door swing open, and unsteadily, he felt his way along the landing, leaning against the wall for support. After what seemed like an hour, but in only a few minutes. Owen finally reached his bedroom.

He felt exhausted, and all he wanted to do was sleep.

On the bed, he closed his eyes and felt uncontrolled tears roll down his face. Within minutes, though, he was snoring deeply.

It was a good job Owen Lyle didn't decide to run down the stairs and run away, as he might have bumped into someone he knew.

Luckily for Owen, a deep sleep took him and he was totally unaware of the elongated shadows lit by the moonlight entering his house.

CHAPTER 48

After she stormed out of the hospital, she sat in her car for a while, trying to calm herself down. Then she headed to the nearest supermarket to get some supplies before heading back to the house.

Owen's time in the hospital would give them some space.

Space she craved at the moment.

On her way home, Freya felt the hurt and wondered how Owen could blatantly lie to her, had looked her in the eye and lied about knowing Lana.

She didn't want to share a bed with him anymore. She'd sleep in the spare room. It was comfortable enough, and she didn't want to sleep in their big bed by herself.

Freya was becoming more and more detached from Owen. And there were two reasons.

His nightmares at first freaked her out and scared her, thinking her husband was going mad. She thought of the dreams she had been having, of the blurred face and the soft voice asking for help.

She hadn't had a dream like that for a few days now. But what scared her was that Owen's nightmares were getting worse. Nightmares through guilt, she thought.

Not a night had gone by without his waking, screaming, or sleepwalking. He called out her name, Lana, but he denied all knowledge of knowing her, having even met her.

Then there was Nathan. How he affected her, how his touch made her tingle all over, and how desperately she wanted him.

But for now, she had to confront Owen. Get him to admit to his affair with Lana. Did he have anything to do with her disappearance, too?

Freya could forgive an affair … nothing else.

Freya arrived home later than she wanted to. Darkness surrounded her as she navigated the bumpy dirt track. The car headlights cast long, eerie shadows across the track. Her heart raced at the thought that someone was going to jump out in front of her. Alone in the middle of nowhere, in the dark, she felt vulnerable.

"Shit." Freya's anger grew as the car's headlights lit up the front of the house and she saw the door was wide open. 'Damn it.' had she forgotten to close the door when the ambulance came? She stopped the car and turned off the engine. As she stepped out of the car, the security light came on, casting a comforting glow in the otherwise dark driveway. 'Thank you, Nathan, for persuading me to install the lights,' she thought to herself. She missed him and wished he was here with her, but she was grateful he wanted to look after Arthur while all this shit with Owen in the hospital was going on.

The wind swirled her hair around her face as she unloaded shopping from the boot of the car.

Halfway to the open front door, the security lights went out. In the sudden darkness, her heart raced, and a dread, a feeling of being watched, came over her. She set her shopping bags down and waved frantically at the sensors, willing the lights to come back on.

At last, the lights flickered and came back on, casting a reassuring glow around her. With relief, she picked up her bags and hurried through the open front door.

As soon as she stepped into the hallway, an uneasy feeling came over her. She dumped the shopping and turned on the lights. They came on but were not as bright as usual. Bulbs were probably on the way out, she assured herself.

'Hello, anyone here?' She looked toward the kitchen and then the lounge. Both doors were closed. 'What the hell?' she stared at the muddy footprints on the floor that went up the staircase.

Suddenly, the house phone rang. The sudden shrill noise erupting over the house almost caused her to pass out.

'Hello.'

'Owen.' she yelled and ran up the stairs, trying to avoid stepping in the muddy footprints.

She didn't know whether she felt anger or fear.

Anger at Owen's inconsiderate behaviour trawling mud up the stairs or fear: Why was he home when he should be in the hospital?

She pushed the bedroom door open to find Owen fully clothed, asleep on top of the covers, gently snoring.

'Owen Lyle, what the hell are you playing at?' she murmured over him. But if the conversation she'd had with Abigail the other day was anything to go by, she knew the answer only too well.

Freya sat on the edge of the bed and stared at her husband.

She was so engrossed in her own thoughts that she didn't notice the two figures behind her disappear from the bedroom.

CHAPTER 49

Last night had been a good night for him. He had slept well, for once, only gently murmuring. She had slept in the same bed only to monitor him.

She decided Owen needed some time off work, and she needed to speak to Alan.

'Hello Freya, how are you?' Alan politely inquired.

'I'm okay, thanks, Alan, but I'm afraid Owen isn't. He discharged himself from the hospital last night, stupid man. Although he slept well last night, he's still shattered. He needs rest. I think staying at home for a few days will help him a lot.'

'Oh, I see. Well, to be honest, Freya, I have noticed how gaunt, worn out and distracted he's been lately, but I'm not surprised. Ever since I showed him the newspaper article on the missing young girl, Lana, he hasn't been himself.'

'Why, for heaven's sake? He's never met her, doesn't know her.' she even convinced herself that this was true.

Alan paused. 'Didn't Owen tell you about her?'

Freya put the receiver in her other hand. 'Tell me what?'

There was an uncomfortable pause from Alan. 'Oh dear, have I put my foot in it?'

'For heaven's sake, Alan, what the hell are you talking about? Owen's having nightmares about the missing woman, and you're about to tell me what about her?'

'Okay, I can understand you're upset and concerned about Owen.' Alan cleared his throat. 'Well, Lana was Owen's intern.' Freya felt the room spin as she slumped onto the sofa. 'What?'

Owen mentioned nothing about him having an intern, ' she stammered down the phone. 'And now she's missing.' It was Freya's turn to pause. 'Was Owen having an affair with her?' Freya said bluntly, knowing exactly the answer, but she wanted to hear it from

Alan, Owen's best friend and boss. But in the pit of her stomach, she already knew the answer Alan would give.

Alan coughed. 'It's against the firm's policy for management to have relations with interns.'

'You've just answered my question, Alan.' Before he could reply, Freya put the phone down and stared at it, not really seeing it. So, it was true. Not that she had doubted Abigail. All the coincidences with Owen from Lana's diary didn't lie.

Lana was Owen's intern. He knew her more intimately than he let on to her. But didn't she already know this, she thought, from Abigail?

A thud from upstairs brought her out of her daze, and she glanced at the ceiling. Freya ascended the stairs, her fingers gripping the handrail and not taking her eyes off the door to her bedroom, where the noise had come from; she could see her breath in the chill air.

Her hand hovered over the door handle. 'Owen.' She whispered. No answer. 'Owen.' Slowly, she opened the door, half expecting to find him on the floor, dead.

No, he lay still in the bed; it was as cold in the bedroom as it was on the landing, and she could see his steady, icy breath in the air.

Freya leaned over him. 'Owen.' She shook him gently, with no response. 'Owen.' She shook him harder.

'Don't worry, he'll be okay.'

A soft voice from behind startled her, and she spun around to find two shadows in the corner of the bedroom as if hiding from the sunlight coming in through the front bedroom window.

'Who's there?' Freya stepped toward the shadows.

One shadow moved closer to Freya.

'I'm sorry, I'm not in the best shape to meet my boyfriend's wife.'

'It's not your fault, Lana.' Another tight, rasping voice filled the room.

The second shadow moved into the light of the room

'Oh, my god!' Freya gaped at the two figures in front of her. 'You're Rose, Spud's mum. I recognise you from the photo he showed me.'

Not sure whether or not to be frightened, Freya still inched away from them.

'Please don't be frightened. We're not here to hurt you.'

'I recognise you, your voice. You're the one I've heard in my head.'

Lana nodded, tufts of dirt dropping from her matted hair.

They stood and checked each other out.

Owen's soft, deep breath was the only noise to break the silence. Freya glanced at her husband, who still looked pale and thin.

'I know you were seeing him, even though you knew he was married.'

Lana bowed her matted head. *'I'm sorry for that. I really didn't know. He lied to me.'*

Sarcastically, Freya said. 'No, but certain people did and turned a blind eye. I didn't know he had an intern. Not a clue. And he lied to me too, telling me he didn't know you and had never met you.'

Lana lifted her head, and in the sudden semi-gloom of the bedroom, Freya recoiled at the decomposing face, at the skin that hung down like rags and the eyes, the dead but sad eyes.

Freya unconsciously put her hand over her mouth and nose from the stench.

'Will you help me?'

'I...I don't understand what's happening here.' Freya finally stammered.

'I don't expect you to because I don't understand either.' Lana's childlike voice hung in the air.

'How is Michael?' The other voice said.

Taken aback, Freya said. 'You mean Spud?'

Freya felt sadness around Rose. Even though her dark hair hung down her face and her shoulders slumped, Freya noticed marks like bite marks on her face and neck. She shuddered at the thought of who she was having a conversation with. Or was she?

'He's sad and misses you so much he thinks he sees you.' Freya said, feeling strangely calm.

Silence filled the room as Owen snorted and shifted a little in bed.

'He has, and he does see me.'

Freya didn't know what else to say, so just stared at the two women.

Lana carried on talking. *'Owen lied to me and you. He murdered me, Freya.'* Her voice rasped from her bruised neck.

Freya quickly glanced at Owen, who was still asleep and oblivious to the two women, the dead women, and her, in the bedroom.

'I want him to admit what he did to me. Did to our baby.'

Freya visibly flinched at Lana's one word. Baby. For a few seconds, she couldn't speak. 'Baby? What do you mean? You were pregnant with Owen's baby?' Freya was stunned at what she just heard.

'Yes.'

Freya stumbled against the window and looked down at the back garden, the cut grass, and the headstone in the far corner. 'Oh, my god.' She felt tears prick her eyes. 'We've been trying for three years for a baby, but I couldn't keep to full term. And now you tell me you are, … were pregnant?'

Freya turned to the women.

'I'm sorry' The sadness in Lana's voice filled the room, and Freya felt a pang of empathy toward her.

'No, you've nothing to be sorry for, Lana. It was all his fault.' She glanced at her sleeping husband. 'And he needs to pay.'

'And he will,'

Freya's attention turned to Rose. 'What do you want, Rose?'

Rose, her head down, said, *'It's time to go. My head hurts.'* Her hand touched the side of her head.

Before Freya's eyes, the two women held hands and seemed to morph into a swirl of mist through the open door, then disappeared like smoke up a chimney.

Owen stirred. 'Freya? What are you doing here?'

'Nothing.' She fled the room. The stench of death permeated her nostrils.

CHAPTER 50

Freya's first thought was to rush and see Abigail. She couldn't keep what she had seen until the next day.

Abigail paced up and down in her apartment, wringing her hands and shaking her head while Freya sat on the sofa with a cold cup of tea on the coffee table in front of her.

'I…I can't believe you saw her.' Abigail stuttered. 'She's dead?'

Freya nodded her head. 'I'm so sorry, Abigail.'

Abigail sat next to her. 'If I'm being honest, I knew it. I knew after all this time she'd be found dead.'

Freya took Abigail's hand in hers. 'We haven't found her yet, her body I mean, have we? Or Spud's mum, Rose.'

'Spud isn't going to like it. Finding out his mum is dead.' Abigail jumped up and looked out the window as a sob escaped her.
'But I think deep down he must know.'

'Lana wants revenge on Owen. I'm not sure what she means?' Abigail sat back down next to Freya and took hold of her hand. 'What can a ghost do? Surely they can't really physically attack people.'

Freya shook her head. 'Who knows? Or maybe she wants me to do something to Owen?' she looked eagerly for answers in Abigail's face. 'After all, he did murder her. And for what? To save his own skin. But it's come back to haunt it, so to speak.'

Abigail nodded. 'Quite the turnaround, isn't it? What about Rose? Who does she want revenge on?'

'She never said, but … well, I'm guessing, Eric.'

'Why Eric?'

'Because Spud thinks Eric knows what happened to his mum, he knows where she is and isn't telling. How cruel is that?'

'There is only one place she could be, where they both could be.'

Abigail nodded. 'Yes. But how are we going to search with Owen hanging around?'

'Leave Owen to me.'

'Do you want me to come with you when you talk to him?' she burst out. 'For moral support, in case he, well, he does something.'

Freya shrugged. 'You mean what happened to Lana? No, I think the last thing we need is Owen seeing us together, his wife and his mistress's friend.' Freya paused. 'I'm sorry. I didn't mean to use that word, especially since I know Owen never told Lana he was married.'

'No need to be sorry. You're right, though; we don't want Owen seeing us together – yet. If what you say, he's becoming unstable.' Abigail suddenly burst out laughing. 'Look at us. Your husband doesn't even realise he's thrown us together, become friends even.' She looked hopefully at Freya.

Freya hugged her. 'Yes, we're friends, Abigail, and we'll get to the bottom of what happened. I promise you that.'

'And make Owen pay?'

'Yes, we'll go to the police and tell them everything.'

'Or maybe not?'

'What do you mean?' Freya saw a twinkle in Abigail's eyes. 'You mean something like in the movies, vigilante-style?'

'Exactly.'

'   CHAPTER 51

The next morning, Owen came downstairs looking sheepish and sat on the sofa without saying a word.

'Start at the beginning, Owen. It's usually the best way, isn't it?' Freya stood in the middle of the living room, glaring at her husband.

'I don't know what you're talking about?'

'Well, if ending up in the hospital with a near heart attack, discharging yourself, and now looking like you are at death's door isn't enough to tell me, I don't know what is. You're not telling me the truth, are you? You had an affair with the missing woman, Lana, didn't you? There, I've said it out loud for you, Owen. That should make it easier for you.'

'Okay, okay, yes I did, and I'm so sorry, I really am. I had an affair, Freya. I wish I could change the past, but I can't.'

Freya crossed her arms. 'So, what happened to her, Owen? What did you do to her?'

'I didn't do anything to her, I swear.'

Freya cautiously sat on the sofa, a distance between them. 'You maintained you never met her, lied to me. So what makes you think I believe you when you say you've done nothing to her?'

'I realised what I was doing was wrong. It was so unfair to you. One minute, I was talking to her calmly, breaking things off with her, and the next thing, she was scratching me, smacking me.' He sighed. 'I saw red and smacked her back hard across her face.' Owen hung his head. 'I'm ashamed of what I did.'

'What part, Owen, having an affair or smacking Lana hard across her face?'

'All of it. When I hit her, she fell backwards and then yelled at me she would call the police, and then she just rushed out of our apartment. I swear, Freya, that was the last time I saw her.'

Freya jumped from the sofa. 'You brought her to our apartment? Did you sleep with her in our bed? You're more of a bastard than I give you credit for.'

'Yes, I'm the biggest bastard going. But I didn't do anything to her. She said she would walk home and told me to … well, fuck off.

That was the last I saw of her. I promise.' He stood and tried to hold Freya.

'Lie, lie, lie. You tried to kill me in the small room at the end of the landing. The room I wanted to turn into a nursery. Why are you not telling your wife the truth, Owen?'

Owen abruptly spun around. 'What? Who said that?'

Freya snorted. 'Oh my god, now you're hearing voices again. How bloody convenient for you to try and stop the question. What did you do to Lana?'

Owen shook her by the arms before she realised what he was doing.

'No, Freya. I heard her; it was her voice. She wants to make me go mad and think it's all in my head, but it isn't. It's her. Tell me it is, Freya, please. I'm begging you.'

Freya shoved him off her. 'You are going crazy, Owen. That's what happens when you murder someone and lie and lie and lie, just to save your own skin.'

Owen, stunned, could only stare at her. 'No. That's not true.'

'Yes, it is, Owen, and you know it. And I know it.' she headed for the living room door.

Suddenly, Owen grabbed her and pinned her against the door.

'I'm telling you, you stupid bitch, I did not kill Lana.' He screamed in her face.

'Oh, but you did.' The sing-song voice whispered in his ear.

Owen staggered backwards, hands clasped on his ears. 'There it is again.' He fell to his knees and wept.

Freya stared at her cowardly husband, unsure what to do.

Against her better judgment, Freya knelt next to him. 'Owen, please tell me the truth. If not for me, for Lana's friend, Abigail.'

Owen turned to face her. 'That bitch.'

The look on his face frightened Freya. The darkness in his eyes and the cruel twist of his mouth left her in no doubt she had better get out of there.

Quickly she scrambled to her feet, but Owen grabbed her leg, and she slammed down on the carpet, just managing to put her hands out to lessen the fall.

Owen crawled over her body to come face to face, his breath on her, and he drooled. 'There is no fucking way I did anything to the stupid kid because that's all she was, a kid, a bit on the side.' He pinned her down.

She kicked at him. 'Get off me, Owen. Let go.'

Struggling, she tried to push him off her, but he was like a dead weight. 'Owen, please.'

He grabbed her hair. 'Please what, Freya? I've done nothing. Maybe been unfaithful, but what the heck? You weren't receptive to my advances, were you?'

'What the hell, Owen? I'd been through two miscarriages.'
Owen, his face inches from hers, just stared down at her. Finally, he slid off her and went to the window and stared out at the woods across the driveway.

Freya wiped the spittle from her face and got to her feet. 'I can't believe how cruel you are.' She hissed. 'You had an affair, Owen. You were shagging someone else while I lost our baby. Not once, but twice. You fucking bastard.' she watched the back of her husband as he just stared out the window, hands in his pockets as if nothing had just happened.

She shivered, not just because of the coldness suddenly enveloping the room, but also because of her anger and hatred towards her husband.

Unexpectedly, Owen turned and laughed at her.

She glanced toward the closed door. 'I'm leaving now.' She sounded calmer than she felt as her heart pounded in her ears.

'Come on, Freya, give me a hug. I forgive your stupidity and ignorance.'

'Don't you touch me,' she pulled the door open.

'I see. You'd rather have the handyman's arms around you, would you? No doubt you've fucked him.'

Freya glared at Owen. 'You are the last person who should question my fidelity. You're a lying son of a bitch. I'll hurt you, Owen.'

Owen laughed. 'Come on, you haven't got it in you.'

The vase that hit him on the side of his head told him otherwise.

CHAPTER 52

Freya filled the kettle and switched it on. While waiting for it to boil, she got one cup and some coffee from the cupboard and thought about what had happened last night.

She was glad the spare bedroom had a lock on the door. Now that everything about Lana was out in the open, she couldn't trust Owen.

His face last night scared her like he was consumed with a hate he couldn't control. He was a liar and a murderer. But she could feel a change in the air. A change that Owen would regret.

Freya stared toward the dark woods for a whole different reason. They didn't scare her anymore. She knew the answer to what was going on. 'Don't you worry about the woods, Arthur. I promise you there's nothing to be frightened of.' Arthur, oblivious, concentrated on the food in his bowl.

The kettle clicked off just as Owen slouched into the kitchen. Freya kept her eyes on him.

'I'm sorry about last night.' Owen said as he touched the side of his head where the vase had hit him.

Freya glared at him, so angry she was shaking. 'You disgust me. I've had enough of you.'

Owen took a step toward her. 'I thought this house would be a new start for us, Freya. I'm trying really hard.'

She turned on him. 'Have you forgotten what happened last night? Seriously?'

'Here we go.' He pulled open a cupboard and yanked out a cup. 'And you're never going to let me forget it, are you?'

'Where has she gone to, Owen? Where has Lana gone? Or shall I put it another way? What have you done to her?'

Owen held his hands up and shrugged, a nonplussed smile on his face. 'You tell me, you seem to know more than me.'

The look on his face disturbed her. 'Stop that, Owen, please.' 'Stop that, Owen, please.' He mocked her.

Freya stormed out of the kitchen. 'Let Arthur out.' She shouted behind her. 'I'm going for a shower.' He heard her footsteps on the wooden staircase and the bathroom door slam.

Owen sat at the table and eyed Arthur, whose tail wagged as he waited to be let out. 'Come on then, Arthur. At least you don't give me grief.' Owen opened the front door and grinned as Arthur headed to the back of the house.

'I don't know why you don't do your business in the woods, there?' Owen said to himself, leaning against the door frame. 'After all, nothing in there would hurt you,'

Suddenly, Owen grabbed hold of the door frame as a wooziness came over him. His body stiffened. He wanted to turn away, to shut the front door and have the woods disappear from his sight, but he couldn't. A force inside him demanded he keep looking.

A dark, angry feeling filled his head, and his throat felt tight; he struggled to breathe. But he couldn't look away from the shape in front of him. The shape of Lana. And who was that beside her?

Owen felt bile rising from his empty stomach, and before he could do anything about it, he spewed all over his trousers.

Catching his breath, Owen blinked rapidly and shook his head to clear the image. The angry feeling quickly left him.

Arthur came bounding back into the house, and with relief, Owen shut the front door.

'Stop.' He moaned in the empty hallway.

He looked up at the landing. The dim light coming through the window.

Freya.

Her name echoed around his head. Her harsh words and threats would only become worse. He knew this. Freya was not a person to forgive so easily. And the last thing Owen Lyle wanted was to be charged with .... Again, his mind couldn't finish the sentence.

Freya was now out to destroy him. She was messing with his head.

She and lover boy were making him see and hear things. They had to be poisoning him. They had to be because there was no such thing as ghosts.

The shock of the memory almost floored him.

'It's an old house, and you know what comes with an old house. Ghosts.'

CHAPTER 53

Spud lay down in the back of the small pickup truck; a blue tarpaulin covered him.

He told Eric he was going to have an early night because he felt under the weather and needed a good night's sleep, and he would appreciate it if Eric didn't disturb him.

Eric and Spud had hardly spoken to each other since Spud had punched Eric, and the festering feeling of hatred wasn't going away. Spud knew Eric was up to something. He wouldn't look him in the eye; he just kept looking out of the kitchen window toward Blyneath.

Spud was determined to find out; tonight would be the night he found his answers. He had a strong feeling Eric would lead him straight to where his mum was, so he crept out of the house and into the back of the truck after Eric had gone to bed.

Even the chilly night didn't put him off, lying in wait for Eric to make his move.

Drifting off, Spud heard the back door open.

He held his breath as Eric climbed into the truck and started the engine. But the truck didn't move.

Eric seemed to wait. For what?

Spud peaked out from under the tarpaulin just as the truck rolled down the driveway.

Spud wasn't sure how long the truck had been on the road, but his head throbbed and his neck ached from the slow, bumpy ride. He was glad when the truck finally came to a stop and the engine turned off.

He heard Eric huff as he got out of the truck and then heard the sound of metal on metal against the side.

Spud lay there, trying to breathe as quietly as he could. He couldn't hear any movement from Eric, only the owls and the woodland nightlife he knew so well out in the sticks.

Out where Blyneath House stood.

After what felt like an hour to Spud but was only five minutes, he thought Eric must have moved away from the truck without him hearing him.

With a slow movement, he lifted the tarpaulin off and peaked over the side of the truck.

Total darkness.

Apart from a small bobbing light moving away from him, deeper into the woods. 'Damn it, should have brought a torch too.' Spud climbed over the side of the truck, trying to make as little sound as possible. He cursed the crunching noise underfoot but kept his eyes focused on the light ahead.

The light was dim, but his eyes soon got used to the darkness,

Eric stopped a little way into the woods. The sounds and darkness were getting to him. It wouldn't bother him under normal circumstances, like when he went poaching. But tonight was different. He felt he was being watched. But by who, he wasn't sure.

Eric wasn't sure about anything anymore.

A snap of a twig from behind him startled Eric. He squinted into the darkness as he tried to make out the shape creeping towards him.

Spud crept up as close as he dared, and when Eric stopped walking to catch his breath, Spud stood still.

The next time Eric stopped, though, he put the torch he had been carrying down on a fallen tree trunk and dug for a few minutes. But he wasn't a young man, and after a while, he sat on the tree trunk to regain his strength.

Taking the torch, he looked around him, moving it in all directions. 'I know you're there, Spud.' Eric turned the torchlight on Spud.

Startled, Spud almost fell backwards into the undergrowth. Regaining his composure, Spud demanded. 'Eric. What are you doing out here?'

Eric sat back down on the fallen tree trunk. 'Come sit with me, Spud. We need to talk.'

'Not sure about that, Eric.' Spud came forward anyway. 'You've got a spade in your hand.'

Eric threw the spade down. 'That better?'

'I've seen what I want to see.' Spud could feel his heart pound in his throat. He knew what was under the soil. But did he really want to see it?

'Follow the torchlight.'

Spud followed the torchlight as it lit the hole in front of Eric's feet.

'I'm sorry.' Eric said as he patted the trunk for Spud to sit next to him.

Hesitating, Spud sat down.

'Is…. she there?' Spud pointed at the hole in the ground.

Eric nodded. Eric looked haunted, lost, and totally drawn out in the torch's light.

'I... I don't know what to say, Eric. I thought I'd be angry, upset, wanting to punch you again, or even worse.'

He tapped Spud on his knee. 'I can understand that.'

'What happens now? With mum.'

Eric chuckled.

'What's so freaking funny, Eric? You've got my mum buried in the dirt.' He jumped up with fists clenched.

Eric grunted as he stood up and put his arm on Spud's shoulder. 'This isn't where your mum is. You know the young woman who's been missing? It's her.'

Spud snatched Eric's torch and aimed it at the hole in the ground. He saw a square yellow piece of fabric and strands of blond hair, and something glinted under the torchlight.

'What the ...?' was all he could say.

Eric brushed through the undergrowth to where he'd chucked the spade and handed it to Spud.

'Put the dirt back, will you, Spud? I'm knackered. Then we'll go home, and I'll tell you everything. I promise.'

'No, Eric, tell me now, how the hell is the missing woman buried on Lyle's property?'

'Because that bastard Owen Lyle is responsible. This is where Owen Lyle buried his bit on the side, and I'm going to make sure he pays for what he's done.'

'I don't understand, Eric. What is going on?'

'Come on, let's get out of this godforsaken wood. It gives the creeps.'

Once in the truck, this time Spud in the front, Eric turned to him. 'Let me just point out, I didn't kill nobody, not the missing girl or your mum.'

Thankfully, the drive back home was in silence.

Spud had too much to think about. Had too much to sink in.

CHAPTER 54

Sleep never came to him that night, and Eric supposed not to Spud, either. Eric had made up his mind about what he was going to do. He would get the hell out of Hartnell, as far away as possible. And as for Spud? Well, he was old enough to look after himself, always had been, Eric admitted.

Eric turned the engine off at the gate where the path led to Blyneath House. The last thing he wanted was for Owen Lyle to know he was coming for him.

Even though he hated it, he walked up to the house in the drizzle. He pulled his hood over his head and zipped up his jacket against the elements.

His footsteps crunched on the gravel driveway, spruced up by Nathan.

'Umm, wonder if he's in? Where's his car?' Part of him hoped Owen wasn't home. Eric wasn't a fan of confrontation.

He hated the house, this place, and everything around it. That night, all those years ago, he wished he had not answered his phone.
His life would have been so different.

But he did, and now he was suffering the consequences.

As he looked up at the house, the rain pelted down and splattered on his face.

Out of the corner of his eye, he saw someone staring at him from the top right window.

Because of the rain splattering on his face, Eric couldn't quite make out who it was. He wiped the rain out of his eyes, then looked up at the window again.

Whoever was there was gone.

The rain seemed to seep through to his bones, and he

shivered. He hesitated at the front door. 'It's about time they repainted this door,' Eric thought as he banged on the peeling, lime-green paint.

His knock reverberated all around him, and the sound unnerved Eric. He couldn't shake the feeling of being watched and twisted to check behind him.

He hoped Owen Lyle would be reasonable to his request, but he wasn't holding his breath. If he didn't get anywhere with this bastard, he would take drastic action. But it was an action he was frightened to take.

Reason being?

There was no doubt in Eric's mind that Owen would fight him and try to implicate him in the murder of Lana Young.

If only he'd decided not to go poaching that day. Another day in his life, he wished he could change. But he couldn't change what had happened. On either day.

If there was any positive outlook on the day Owen murdered the young woman, it is that Eric had managed to lead him away from the one burial place Eric didn't want to see, didn't want to remember. He banged on the door again and was about to leave.

'Who is it?' a gruff voice shouted behind the front door.

'Owen Lyle, is that you?'

'Who is it?'

Eric gulped at the anger in the voice. 'It's me, Eric. Eric, the removal man and...' he stopped himself from completing the sentence. 'Your accomplice?' he thought.

The door flung open, and Owen stood with just his trousers on. His hair dishevelled, as if he had been asleep.

'Hi, Owen. We need to talk.' Eric hoped he sounded like he meant business.

'About what? What the hell have I got to say to you?' Owen brushed his hand through his hair. 'Leave me alone. I've nothing to say to the likes of you.'

'Eric. My name is Eric. Oh, and by the way, good acting skills when you pretended not to remember my name at the gate when we arrived with all your belongings. Nice touch, that was.'

'I'll say this once more. What do you want?' Owen swayed forward and backwards with his left hand on the doorknob, taking the door with him.

Eric noticed the bags under Owen's eyes and the grey pallor of his skin, and he looked like he'd lost a lot of weight.

'Are you okay?' Eric said.

'What do you care?'

Eric put his foot on the threshold to stop Owen from slamming the door in his face. 'At least invite me in, Owen. It's raining pretty hard now, and I'm soaked.' He looked up towards the sky as if to make his point.

'I don't give a shit.'

'Okay, but I think we have a lot to talk about.' From inside his jacket, Eric produced a newspaper and held the front page in front of Owen's face.

Owen laughed, 'Come on, Eric, that's old news.'

'I don't think so. I need money, you arsehole. I'll go to the police with what I know.'

Owen stepped towards Eric, forcing him to back out of his way.

'And what do you know, you piece of shit? Seeing as we're calling each other names.' He laughed again.

'I saw what you did with that missing woman.' Eric stood his ground.

'I might just add, Eric, that you did nothing to help her, did you? Just stood and watched.'

'I couldn't believe what I was seeing, a murder right in front of me.'

'You should have stayed where you were, but no, you had to come out of your hiding place, all flustered and holier than thou at what you saw, and may I remind you, Eric, you were poaching on my land.'

It was Eric's turn to laugh. 'Hah. It wasn't your land then.'

'But it is now, so get off my land.'

'I mean it, Lyle. I want money, or I'll go to the police.'

'And say what? That you witnessed a murder, and you did nothing to help her?' Owen slammed his right hand against the door, making Eric jump. 'Oh, yes, you did do something to help her, didn't you, Eric?'

Eric shuffled his feet. 'I had no choice. You forced me.'

'And why was that, Eric? Let me tell you, shall I? You were poaching, and you couldn't afford to get arrested; you would have done jail time. You know, I've always wondered why. Why would you help me bury a body? Something I think is more serious than poaching going on with you. Am I right?'

'I had my reasons then. But things have changed.' An image of Rose sprawled on the grass in the pouring rain broke into his mind, and he shivered.

Owen stepped outside, the canopy over the front door keeping the rain off him.

'How?'

'I'm not scared of you, Lyle.' Eric so wanted to make his way back down the driveway, back down the track, back to the safety of his truck.

'I'll give you two days to get ten thousand pounds together. Or else.'

Owen stepped out into the rain and followed him. 'Or else what?' The rain dripped from his hair onto his chest.

'I will go to the police.'

Eric didn't see the punch to his nose coming. He fell flat on his back.

'Let's get one thing straight, shall we? No one....'
Suddenly, a screech came from the woods. Eric and Owen sharply turned toward the noise.

'What the hell was that?' Eric scrambled to his feet and felt the blood drain from his face as he peered into the shadows, into the darkness of the wood.

He had never heard such a primal, deep, pained sound, and he stood frozen, looking from the woods to Owen.

Eric knew he should run and return to the safety of his dull existence before he ever met Owen Lyle.

Owen pushed past Eric and scanned the woods in front of him. 'Come out, don't mess with me,' Owen glared into the darkness of the wood. 'Whoever you are, I've had enough of your games. Stop messing with me. Come out NOW.'

The tension in the air was heavy as Owen's voice echoed around them.

And the trees swayed in the pouring rain; the sound came again, this time nearer.

Then another sound, softer, like whispers, whispers of… neither could make out the words if there were words to be heard.

Owen shivered, crossed his arms over his bare chest against the cold, and eyed a shocked Eric.

Eric could see the veins in Owen's neck throbbing.

Abruptly, the wind stopped, but the trees still swayed in front of them. A loud crack echoed around them like a tree trunk breaking in two.

The whisper, the deep growl, sounded nearer.

Owen raged closer to the sound. 'I'm warning you.'

'Lyle.'

'Who the hell is in the woods, MY woods?' Owen, drenched, marched toward the noise.

'Lyle,' Eric couldn't help but scream.

'What the hell, Eric?' Owen swirled around to see Eric's outstretched, shaking hand pointing in the same direction he had been headed for.

'Can't you see it? The legs?'

Owen turned back at the dark expanse of the wood and stared. Eric was right. There in front of them was a pair of skinny, grimy legs.

Owen's eyes ran up the legs towards the body that belonged to them. He quickly scrambled back to Eric. 'Shit, Eric, I can't see who it is?' He grabbed Eric by the arm.

'Are you sure, Lyle?' Eric peeled Owen's hand from his arm.

'For fuck's sake, Lyle, look at the dress.'

Owen could clearly see what was in front of him, and he didn't want to see the person who stood there in the darkness watching them, watching him. The rain fell harder, and he was grateful the rain blurred his vision.

'Don't you recognise the dress?' Eric shouted above the noise of the pounding rain.

Owen shivered. 'No. There's no one there.'

Eric couldn't believe what Lyle was saying to him. He looked back toward the woods.

Lyle was right, there was no one there. Now.

An enraged Owen grabbed Eric by his jacket and hauled him to the end of the driveway. 'I told you no one is in the bloody woods. Now fuck off, Eric and I don't want to see you again.'

He shoved Eric so hard that Eric nearly fell onto the muddy track.

251

Breathless, Eric watched Owen as he splattered barefoot through the puddles, back to his house, stomped inside, and slammed the front door shut.

Eric stared at the closed door for a few seconds before returning his gaze to the spot where he was sure he'd seen those legs. There was nothing but darkness.

But Eric knew what he saw, and what he saw frightened him. He had neglected to point out to Owen, on purpose, the other pair of legs he'd seen, a faded pink flowered dress clinging to them.

Eric's heart raced, and he grabbed his chest. He couldn't think straight as the memory of another poor decision he'd made came flooding back.

The pink flowered dress was unmistakable.

It was the same dress she had worn when they buried her.

Eric forced himself to pull his gaze away from the woods and tentatively walked back down the track. Resisting the temptation to look back at the house or the woods.

CHAPTER 55

The constant banging at the front door reverberated through the house and irritated Owen. He was cold and still shivered, no matter how many layers he wore. No matter how many layers he wore, he couldn't get warm. This morning with Eric had made him angry, and he ached all over. And shuffling to answer the front door made him angry.

'I'm coming.' He coughed, trying to catch his breath. 'Who the bloody hell is there, and what the shit do you want?'

As soon as the door creaked open, Spud stopped banging on the door. 'Mr Lyle! I wasn't expecting you to be here.' Spud nervously stepped away from the door.

'What?' Owen squinted at him. 'Oh, it's you, the little shit that wouldn't do the job I paid for.'

Spud shuffled his feet. 'I need to see Freya. Is she home?'

'Why the hell do you want to see my wife?'

Spud glanced behind Owen into the hallway. The house was in semi-darkness. The light from the kitchen was dull, and the lamp at the top of the stairs hardly gave out any light.

'I have something to tell her, that's all.'

'What.' Owen leaned against the front door. 'I'll give her a message, or you can come in and wait.'

Spud stepped back. 'No, I'll call back later.'

Startled, when Owen grabbed his arm and pulled him into the hallway, Spud let out a yelp.

'Come on, I've not seen you for a while. I'm sorry I was rude just then.'

Owen coughed so badly that Spud thought he might pass out.

Owen slammed the front door shut.

'Mr Lyle, I don't need to come into the house.'

He pulled Spud toward the kitchen. 'Nonsense. Come on, have a drink.'

'I don't want a drink.'

Suddenly, Owen was in Spud's face, and he could feel the coldness of his breath. Gripping hard, he pulled Owen's hand from his arm and stepped away. 'I said no.'

'If it weren't for your little prank when we moved in here, my wife would be none the wiser.' Owen spat.

'None the wiser about what?' Spud edged his way back to the front door.

'Don't give me that crap. You know what I'm talking about. Your uncle Eric, I bet he told you about me, didn't he? After this morning's little prank, he sent you, didn't he? Get money out of me.'

'I have to go.' Owen's look unnerved Spud. He fumbled for the door handle, pulled the front door open with all his strength, and scrambled outside.

'Come on, Spud, that's your name, isn't it? Hell, what kind of name is that, anyway?'

'I know what you did to Lana.' Spud stuttered at Owen. 'We all do.'

Owen snorted. 'What did I do, Spud? Go on, tell me.' Owen stepped closer to him. 'And who are 'we all'?'

Spud, eyes wide and his breath coming quickly, glanced around him. The sky above suddenly took on a sombre grey, and he shivered as the coldness he felt in the house seemed to have followed him outside.

The wind picked up and swirled fallen leaves around him.

From the corner of his eye, Spud thought he saw movement between the trees, like someone trying not to be seen.

Spud didn't like it one bit. He desperately wanted to run. Run away from the evil he felt surrounded this place.

'We know. And you're not going to get away with it.'

Owen stepped over the threshold and out into the dusk of the sky. 'Get away with what, Spud?'

Spud backed away. Owen frightened him. He turned and ran down the driveway, only stopping when he thought there was enough distance between them.

He watched Owen shuffle back into the house. 'I did nothing wrong.' Owen barked. With that, the door slammed shut.

Shocked by Owen's reaction as he walked further away from the house, Spud thought it strange that even though the afternoon sun had some warmth, inside the house, it was cold—so cold he could see

Mr Lyle's breath.

But the strange thing was, Spud thought, he couldn't see his own.

CHAPTER 56

Nathan waited for Freya in the coffee shop in Hartnell. He was early and on his second cup of coffee he was that eager to see her.

Early morning, Freya had called him at home. She sounded like an excited child, and he couldn't understand what she was saying, only that she'd meet him in the coffee shop in Hartnell.

The bell over the door of the coffee shop tinkled, and Nathan was relieved to see this time, it was Freya with Arthur, who pulled on his lead towards Nathan in his eagerness to see him.

While Arthur made himself comfortable at Nathan's feet, Freya took off her coat.

He admired her ability to remove her coat and hat and order a coffee in one fell swoop. But Nathan had started to admire everything Freya did.

Almost.

He didn't admire the fact Freya kept giving her husband the benefit of the doubt.

There was no doubt in his mind what kind of man Owen Lyle really was.

'So, what's so important?' he asked.

Freya plonked herself in the chair opposite him and leaned towards him. She grabbed his hands in hers and squeezed.

'I've seen her.' Freya grinned.

Nathan shrugged. 'Seen who?'

'I've seen Lana. Spoken to her.' Freya glanced around the coffee shop to see if anyone had heard her.

No one was paying her any attention.

Nathan realised his mouth was open and quickly closed it.

'You talked to her? So she's okay?'

'Umm, not quite.'

'What do you mean, not quite? You've seen her, right, so she must be okay?'

'She's dead. But I did see her.' Freya held her excitement out of her voice.

'I'm confused here.' he reluctantly pulled his hands from hers. 'She's dead, but you saw her? So how did that come about, then?'

A breathless Freya was in a rush to get her words out. 'She came to me. I had phoned Alan, Owen's boss, to tell him Owen was not well, still having nightmares, and he needed to have some time off work to rest up. Then he told me Owen had been upset about the missing girl, and that's when Alan let slip Lana was an intern for Owen. Well, I tell you something, Nathan, I was gobsmacked. Owen never said a word to me about her. Apart from lying to me about her.'

'The bastard. Sorry.' Nathan held his hands up in an apology.

'Hey, no, you're right, he is a bastard, so is Alan. I asked him if Owen was having an affair, and he told me, I quote, it's against the firm's policy for management to have relations with interns. What do you think about that then?'

Leaning in, Nathan said. 'So, what are you going to do now? About Owen, I mean? Knowing he blatantly lied to you?'

'Wow, Nathan, I thought you'd be more freaked out about me seeing a dead person, a ghost.' Freya stared at him.

'An alleged ghost.' Nathan realised he'd said the wrong thing. 'I didn't mean it like that,' he backtracked. 'What I mean is, you've been under a lot of stress, and maybe you just, erm, might have …' Nathan stopped talking when he noticed the hard line of her lips.

He hadn't known her very long, but he did recognise her look of annoyance.

Freya's face softened. 'No, you have a point, I guess. But I know what I saw, Nathan, it was Lana. The smell alone makes me know she was there.' Freya paused when the waitress placed her coffee in front of her. 'I've been to see Abigail to tell her about Lana.'

'Abigail?'

Without thinking, Freya rubbed Nathan's hands as if to warm them up. 'I thought I told you about her. She's Lana's best friend, the one that reported her missing to the police.'

'I see. My hands are nice and toasty now. Thanks, Freya.' Nathan smiled and withdrew his hands.

Freya blushed.

The bell over the door tinkled, and they both looked up to see a troubled-looking Spud headed straight for them.

'And Rose was with her.' Freya quickly said before Spud could take a seat.

CHAPTER 57

Angered by Spud's unwelcome visit, Owen tried to light a fire in the living room and get some warmth into his bones. 'Why is it so damn cold?' He put more wood on the fire and bent into the flames, and rubbed his hands to warm them.

A door bang suddenly echoed around the house. Owen stiffened. Footsteps echoed through the hallway, getting closer and closer. He squeezed his eyes shut as if this would make the footsteps stop.

They did.

He reluctantly opened his eyes. 'Hello.' His voice quivered as the fire crackled behind him.

'Owen?'

'No, please leave me alone.' He yelled into the room.

'Owen, it's me, Alan.'

Owen blinked, trying to take in the voice. 'Alan? You're here?' a sob escaped from Owen. 'Oh my god, you are.'

Alan took Owen's arm and guided him onto the sofa. 'My god, Owen, what the hell has happened to you? You look dreadful.'

Eventually, Owen managed to get Alan into focus. 'It's you, it's really you.' he grabbed hold of Alan and hugged him.

Alan could feel Owen's body shake. 'Owen, calm down.' Alan gently pushed Owen's arms from his shoulders.
Freya was right, you're not well at all. She said you are still having nightmares. Is that true?'

Owen sobbed. 'Bitch. She hates me. She thinks I murdered someone.'

Alan shuffled along the sofa to take in Owen and stared at his friend. 'Who thinks you murdered someone, Owen?'

Abruptly, Owen sprang from the sofa and paced around the lounge. 'Freya, that's who. Are you stupid? She thinks I murdered

Lana, that slut, that intern you forced on me.' Owen pointed an angry finger at Alan.

'Shit.' Alan muttered.

Owen stopped in mid-stride. 'Shit what, Alan.' He glared at him.

'Look, I'm sorry, but Freya phoned me and told me you wouldn't be at work for a few days, that you needed some rest because of your nightmares, keeping you sleep-deprived and driving you crazy.'

Owen stared at Alan. 'She phoned you?'

Alan undid his tie and the top button of his shirt. 'It's hot in

here.'

'What did you say to her, Alan?'

'Err… I did mention you weren't yourself since I showed you the picture of Lana.' Alan shuffled uncomfortably in his seat.

'And?'

Alan coughed. 'Well, I did let it slip that Lana was an intern of yours and…'

The next thing Alan knew, he was sprawled on the floor, blood oozing from his nose.

'Owen, what the hell?' Alan tried to shove Owen off him.

'What else did you say, you piece of shit? What?' he grabbed Alan to his feet.

With all his strength, Alan shoved Owen off him. Shaking, he pointed at Owen. 'What the hell, Owen? Freya was right, you're not well, you're not thinking straight.'

'WHAT DID YOU TELL MY WIFE?'

'She knows Lana was your intern.'

Alan was too slow. Owen knocked him to the ground. His fists pummelled his head again and again.

Alan scratched at Owen and tried to push him off. 'Owen, Stop, please.' He gasped.

'NO, NO, NO. It's your fault I had to confess to Freya about Lana. Why couldn't you keep your mouth shut?' Owen sobbed as his fist impacted Alan's face, his head hitting the floor with an almighty crunch.

Breathing deeply and with sweat running down his face, Owen staggered off Alan.

He stood there for a few minutes, staring at the blood spreading on the floor. 'Get up, you piece of shit.' He said as he kicked

Alan's foot in disgust.

Alan didn't move. Owen knelt and shook Alan's shoulder. No response. 'Shit.' Owen jumped up and ran to the door.

Darkness was on the horizon. It was still. And quiet. No wind. No rain. His breath came quickly and icily in the looming darkness when he noticed Alan's car in the driveway.

Back in the lounge, Owen searched Alan's pockets for the car keys. Finding them, he put them in his trouser pocket, then grabbed hold of Alan's ankles and dragged him out of the house. He didn't care when Alan's shirt rode up his back and the gravel scratched it, nor when Alan's head thudded on the gravel driveway.

Unceremoniously, he shoved Alan onto the back seat and climbed into the driver's seat. He started the engine and drove the car back down the driveway.

Just before the rotten gate, Owen stopped the car. He sat there for a moment, the engine ticking over, and gazed at the woods to his left, then to his right.

What was he doing? He thought, then through the rearview mirror, he saw Alan's lifeless body. Alan, the traitor who had told his wife he was ... no, he thought, had an affair with Lana.

With grim determination, Owen pulled Alan from the car. His dead weight made it hard for him to drag him into the woods a few feet away, where a hole was already dug.

In the encroaching darkness, he could hardly see what he was doing, but he was used to the darkness now and knew the woods pretty well. Owen had spent enough time in them, wondering through them when he could, to find the right spot.

He didn't want to dig near the other one.

The other hole.

With one last push, Alan's body thudded into the hole. Owen shovelled the best he could with his bare hands, covering up the body.

Now he had to get rid of Alan's car. Owen drove the car as far as he could into the woods. Branches scratched and smacked against the new car until the car came to a halt. It would have to do for now, Owen thought.

'Freya Lyle, you don't know how lucky you are tonight.'

CHAPTER 58

Spud rushed to their table and sat down on the spare chair. 'I've just been to your house, Freya, to see if you were there, to talk to you, but obviously you're here.' he shrugged. 'Anyway, Owen opened the door and dragged me inside. He's not well, Freya, and when I say that I mean he's crazy.' He let out a long-held breath.

'What do you mean? Has he hurt you?' concerned, Freya touched his arm.

Spud patted her hand. 'No, I'm okay, really. But your husband clearly isn't,'

Freya glanced at Nathan. 'Something needs to be done, and quickly.' He said.

Abruptly, Freya stood. 'I have to go home.'

'No. We have to think about this. Please, sit down, Freya. It sounds like he's losing it. He might even hurt you?' Nathan pleaded.

'Owen would never hurt me.' Freya looked between Spud and Nathan. She knew it was a lie, but she would not admit to Nathan what Owen had already done to her. She knew he would go straight to her house and have it out with Owen and maybe even beat him up.

No matter how much Owen deserved it, she didn't want Nathan getting into trouble.

'Are you sure about that?' Nathan stared hard at Freya.

'Come to my house. It's quiet and no one will interrupt us.'

'What about Eric?' Freya said. 'Won't he be there?'

'I don't know what's up with Eric, but he seems to spend a lot of time in his room, sleeping. He won't disturb us.' Spud was out the door before either could say a word.

Freya put on her coat and reluctantly nudged a sleeping Arthur from under the table. 'I'll ring Abigail,' she said.

After hearing what the three had to say, Abigail sat silently for a few minutes. 'I knew it. At least Owen confessed to seeing her. I'm surprised Lana could do things like haunting, get into his head, and make him do things. She is … was, a timid person. There is no way she'd be capable of, what did you call it, Freya, revenge?.'

Nathan sat at Spud's kitchen table. 'I'm sorry about your friend, Abigail. Now, I don't pretend to have a clue about the afterlife, ghosts or whatever else there is out there. Maybe they become, I don't know, more the person they wanted to be when they were alive.' A deathly silence filled the room.

'My mum,' Spud quietly said.

They all looked at him, then at each other.

'Eric told me he didn't know where my dad had buried my mum. But he does. The coward just can't tell me. I don't know why?'

'Let me guess.' Freya said. 'Blyneath.'

Spud didn't know if he should tell them where Lana was buried. Maybe this wasn't the time or place.

If anyone needed to know, it was Abigail; he wouldn't blurt it out. He'd tell her when she was on her own. But first, he needed to talk to Freya alone.

Spud nodded and heaved himself onto the worktop, the only other space in the small kitchen. 'Remember me telling you, Freya, about my visions, about me seeing my mum? But they faded. Then you moved in, and the visions and dreams became stronger. More real, more powerful.'

Freya nodded in understanding. 'I think we need to end this.' 'How?' Spud said.

'First, we need to get Owen to confess he murdered her and get him to tell us where exactly in the woods did he bury her?' Abigail banged on the table. 'Sorry.' She said when she saw Spud's raised eyebrows.

'I sort of already told Owen that we know about him and Lana.' Spud rubbed his arms and looked at the floor.

'What?' Nathan said.

'You mean you've told him about all of us knowing? He now knows it's not just me and Abigail accusing him of murder.'

'I was scared, okay? He had this wild look on his face, and I panicked. I wanted to stop him in his tracks.' 'Did it work?' Nathan sarcastically said.

'Of course not.' Spud looked up at Nathan.

'Sorry, Spud. I didn't mean to sound so…'

'Stupid?' Freya glared at Nathan. 'Well, if Owen knows, we know. I don't think he'll be bothered about doing something dreadful.'

'I think he's already done something dreadful, don't you?' They all looked at Abigail.

'Still think Owen wouldn't hurt you?' said Nathan.

Freya looked out of the kitchen window.

On the landing, Eric listened to the conversation taking place in his kitchen. His nephew was no longer under his control or afraid of him, and he didn't like it.

These people believed Spud and were influencing him to think for himself. They were willing to help him, at any cost, find where he and Seth had buried his mum.

Eric was scared. Since he visited Owen to get money from him and saw what he'd seen in the woods, he couldn't bring himself to face the world or Spud. Because if he did, he would end up confessing everything.

Even though Eric felt Rose's death wasn't his fault, he knew he should have done something about Seth.

Made Seth pay for what he did to his beloved Rose and go to the police, as he should have all those years ago.

But Eric had been weak. He had let his brother bully him into helping him dispose of Rose like a bag of rubbish by scaring him into thinking Spud would be left alone.

Had Seth known all along about Spud? Was that why Seth could so easily manipulate him?

Now was the time to get a backbone. He wasn't going to prison, not now, not never. This time he would stand his ground and fight for himself for a change.

He had to stop the major culprit in all of this.

Freya Lyle.

'You leave her alone, Eric.'

He spun around so fast he almost smashed his face into the wall.

He knew that voice.

'Rose?' he whispered. 'Is that you?'

'*Leave her alone,*'

Tears fell, and he slid down the wall. 'Was that you I saw in the woods, Rose?'

A hotness spread down his cheek.

'*Leave her alone.*'

A breath on his face, he could smell decay and roses. He could smell his piss as it flowed into the carpet.

CHAPTER 59

After their talk at Spud's house, Freya wanted to dig up the woods. As she was coming around from the back of the house, with Arthur in tow, Spud was walking up her drive.

'Spud, what a lovely surprise.'

'Freya, I've something to tell you. I didn't want to say anything in front of Abigail yesterday.' He looked around him. 'Nathan here?'

'No, he went into the city to check out the land registry for this place and see if there was something on it that showed the headstone and why it was here.'

'Good move. And Mr Lyle?' Spud couldn't help his nervousness as he glanced at the open front door.

'Crazy man's hauled himself into work. I can't stand him around me anymore, so I wasn't going to stop him.'

'Well, I might be able to help you there.'

Freya put the spade down. 'Come inside, Spud, I'll put the kettle on.'

He followed her and Arthur into the house with a quick glance at the woods he had been into the other night.

'By the way, Spud, how do you feel about coming into the house now?'

Taken aback at the blunt question, Spud realised he felt different from the first time.

'I ...I actually feel calm.' He nodded. 'I don't know why, but I feel calm. I feel calm with you. I'm not afraid anymore.'

'Wow, Spud, that's amazing. Why the change?' she smiled at him.

All Spud could do was shrug. He stared out into the woods.

'Maybe it's to do with what I have to tell you about what happened with me and Eric the other night out in the woods.' He pointed.

'What? You were on my property?'

'I'm sorry. I was following Eric.'

The screech of an engine caught Spud and Freya's attention.

'What the heck?' Spud watched from the kitchen window as the truck came to a halt inches from the front door.

Surprised, they watched Eric jump from the truck and march toward them. Without knocking, he stormed into the house and headed for the kitchen, where Freya and Spud were.

Eric stood in front of Spud, his face red with rage and his eyes bulging. 'Why, why, Spud?'

'Eric, get out of my face, so I swear.'

Arthur started barking at Eric.

Freya stepped between them, holding them apart. 'What the hell, Eric? What's the matter with you?'

'I'm sick of you, Spud. Why are you here with her? Why are you always talking to her?' Eric pointed a shaky finger at Freya. 'I've told you the truth. I don't know where Seth took her.'

'Why do you have a problem with me talking to Freya? At least she listens to me, not make fun of me. Anyway, this time, it's not just about my mum.'

'It's all rubbish. Rubbish, that's what comes out of your mouth, Spud. Rubbish.'

'Are you sure about that, Eric?' Freya stared hard at him. 'Because I know the truth.'

'Remember the other night, out in the woods, eh, Eric?'

Eric stumbled against the cupboards.

Suddenly, Eric burst into tears, leaned over the kitchen sink, and sobbed. After a few seconds, with his composure returning, he turned to Spud. 'Your mum's been rotting in the ground for 20 years, Spud. Twenty fucking years.' he suddenly burst out laughing like a hyena.

Spud took a step towards Eric, his fists clenched. 'What do you mean?' Spud spat.

Standing beside him, Freya put a hand on his arm to stop him.

'Are you stupid, boy?'

Spud flinched, and the memory of his father calling him that time and time again came flooding back. He could do no right in his dad's eyes.

'Did you hear what I just said? Your beloved mum has been rotting, decomposing, keeping the worms and whatever else alive.' Eric slumped down on a chair, head in his hands. He looked up into

Spud's hurt face. 'And I think about that night every single day.'

Spud spoke so softly and calmly. 'I know my mum's dead, Eric, and I know Seth had a part in that. What I want to know is your part in the death of my mum, and where she is?'

271

Eric scraped the chair back across the tiled floor as he stood. He gazed out of the kitchen window at the woods. The trees stood to attention as if waiting for him to tell his tale, waiting for him to unleash the burden he'd been carrying around with him all these painful years, waiting for the truth.

'I loved your mum so much, Spud. I think she loved me too when we were together, at least. Then Seth turned up from his worldwide wonderings, and he turned her head. Filled her head with lies about where he'd been and where he was going to take her one day.'

Eric glanced over his shoulder to Spud, whose face was disbelieving.

'You were with my mum first?'

Eric nodded. He shuffled to the kitchen door as if to leave.

'Yes.'

'What happened, Eric?' said Freya.

'I guess Rose wanted a bit of excitement, but she felt like she wasn't getting it from me. Seth had the gift of the gab, you see. He could have had anyone, but he took my Rose from me.' he ached. 'In more ways than one.'

'What do you mean by that?' Freya glanced at Spud. Confusion was all over his face.

'Seth took away the most precious thing I ever had and ruined it. I hated him for it. I hated him,' he stared at the floor.

'Is that why you never came to the house?' Spud said. 'But you came when he called you for help. Why?'

Spud shuddered at his uncle's pained, haunted expression.

Eric felt a twinge in his chest. 'Seth claimed it was an accident. Rose hit her head when she slipped on the wet grass, trying to get under the trees to shelter from the rain.' Eric sighed. 'I didn't want to help Seth. I went to help Rose. He took me to where Rose was lying. I could see straight away that you don't get bruises on your face, a bust lip if you fall and hit your head.' Eric wiped a stray tear from his cheek. 'I could tell she was dead.'

'Thanks to your brother.'

Eric sharply looked out into the hallway. Rose, he thought, how can she be here? No, he imagined her voice. Just like before.

Freya shivered. 'It's got cold in here.'

'So, where is my mum, Eric?'

'I'm here.'

'What the...' Eric scrambled next to Freya, his face ashen white. 'No, you're not here.' he grabbed Freyas's arm.

'Eric, let go. You're hurting me.' she peeled his fingers from her arm.

'Did you hear that.... that.' Eric garbled.

Spud stood at the kitchen door and looked out into the hallway. 'What's the matter, Eric? You hear voices or something?'

Eric lunged toward Spud and grabbed him by his shirt. 'Don't play games with me, boy. How did you do that?'

Spud pulled Eric's hands off him. 'Do what? Eric, what is the matter? What's going on?'

Eric stumbled back against the kitchen sink. 'I'm leaving.' He pushed past Spud, who grabbed him.

'Eric, you're not leaving until you tell me exactly where my mum is.'

Freya squeezed past them into the hallway. She turned to Eric. 'Where is Spud's mum?'

Eric pushed them both aside and made for the front door. He lunged at the handle, turning it and trying to open it.

'I'm sorry, Spud. I really am, but I can't stay here because she....' a force slammed him against the front door.

'Tell him.'

'NO!' Eric screamed as he slid down the door. "Please, no, let me go." His eyes rolled back. Eric clutched his chest and curled up, wracked with pain. His breath came out in rasps.

Freya ran to him. 'Eric.' She shook him, 'Eric.' She turned to Spud, who could only stare open-mouthed at his uncle on the floor as he gasped for air. Mid-gasp, he stopped, and his eyes came down from his sockets. Spud stared into the haunted dead eyes of his uncle.

To the left of the hallway, a shadow caught Spud's eye. Slowly, he turned and saw a ball of mist swirling at the bottom of the stairs, hovering like it was waiting. Waiting for something or someone.

'Spud.'

The voice sounded tinny and far away. He wasn't sure if he heard what he heard. His name being called.

'Spud.' The shaking of his arm got his attention. Freya stood in front of him. 'Spud, we have to call an ambulance.' Freya followed Spud's gaze towards the staircase. 'What is it?'

Spud sluggishly turned to Freya. 'It's cold in here, isn't it?'

Whisper Of Ghosts

CHAPTER 60

Spud looked down at the coffin. Around the graveside stood Freya,

Nathan, and Abigail. And Arthur. Freya wouldn't leave Arthur alone with Owen anymore.

There was no one else that mattered to him.

He held a letter in his hand: 'Eric left this for me on my bed before he came to your house, Freya.'

Freya touched his arm. 'What does it say?'

Spud took a deep breath. 'Eric was my father.'

Abigail, Freya, and Nathan looked at each other in disbelief.

'No, I couldn't take it in either.'

'I'm sorry, Spud, I really am.' Abigail linked her arm to his, and Spud led her away from the graveside.

Freya and Nathan fell in step with them.

'My mum was pregnant with me. She was about to tell Eric she was pregnant when Seth came on the scene. Apparently, Eric had nothing to offer her, and when Seth told her tales of his life abroad, all the places he'd been to and all the exciting people he'd met, she fell for his tall tales.' Spud took a deep breath. 'My mum thought Seth would be the one to take her away from her dull life.' he shrugged.

'But it turned out to be all lies, and Mum never found out until after they were married.

Her father practically held a gun to Seth's head when he found out his little princess was pregnant. Mum was upset that

Eric had moved on with someone else. Although Eric says in his letter that he never found anyone else. It was Seth who made it all up.'

'Wow, Spud, I'm sorry.' Nathan patted him on his back. 'If there's anything I can do.'

'Thanks.' Spud turned to Freya. 'What about your husband, Freya?'

'What do you mean?'

Spud looked down at the letter in his hands. 'There's more than that in the letter. The rest is for you. I know what's in it. It's not pleasant reading, and I'm sorry.'

Freya felt the blood drain from her face as she took the letter from Spud. 'It's about Owen, isn't it?'

Spud nodded. 'I think you always knew, deep in your gut, there was an actual reason your husband decided to up sticks and move away from the city without consulting you, without giving you any concrete reason.'

'Nathan, I don't want to read it.' she passed it to him.

'Look, I'll leave you to read. Call me if you need to please.' Spud bent and tickled Arthur. Then, without a backward glance, he and Abigail walked through the gate and out of the cemetery.

'Shit.' Freya turned to Nathan. 'Let's get out of here. It gives me the creeps, graveyards.' Arthur happily walked between Freya and Nathan.

'And headstones.' Nathan took her hand. 'I couldn't find anything from the land registry about headstones or anything else.' The sky darkened as if sensing the impending events that would unfold. 'The headstone now has two more letters. I didn't want to tell you before.'

Freya stopped. 'What other letters? How's that possible?'

He held her hand and then said. 'The other letters are O and A.'

'So now the headstone has an L, E, O, and A carved into it?'

'Yes, but that's the least of our problems at the minute. What are we going to do about Owen?' he asked apprehensively.

After a few seconds of silence, she whispered, 'Something has to be done.'

CHAPTER 61

Owen couldn't face the stares and the questions about Alan. The accusing looks from work colleagues. He wished he could blow up the building and send them all to hell. So he left, leaving behind a mess of papers and unanswered questions.

He slouched on the sofa, whisky in hand, and jolted as the front door slammed. 'Okay, I know you're mad, but please don't slam the fucking door. I've got a headache and don't need the grief of you starting an argument.' No answer.

'Freya.'

Silence.

'Fuck off then. I'm sick and tired of you thinking I had anything to do with Lana's disappearance. Bloody hell, she was sleeping with anybody that gave her attention. I'm in the clear here.'

'Sure you are.'

Owen twisted off the sofa, onto his hands and knees, then staggered to his feet.

'Come on now. Freya. Freya.' He shouted. 'Stop messing with me.'

'I'm the one messing with you.'

Owen bent double as the pain in his chest took hold. 'Go away.' He tried to scream as an unseen hand touched his face.

'Owen, admit you murdered me.'

Owen staggered backwards as he stared at the sight of his mistress. 'Why are you doing this to me?'

'*Hello, Owen.*' Lana stepped forward. She looked alive and well; her blonde hair flowed down her shoulders, and her blue eyes sparkled.

'*Look.*' she said, cradling her baby bump. '*Look, I'm beginning to show.*' Lana smiled at Owen as she stepped toward him.

'You're not real. It's a trick, that's it, that's what's happening here, I know it is.' He stammered.

'*Owen, I know you're scared, but I'm here for you.*'

Owen scrambled out of the living room into the hallway. Shaking, he stared at the scene in front of him.

Lana seemed to float toward him, arms outstretched. She leaned into him, but this time, her hair was lank and her body thin and rotten. Dried blood caked her legs.

Owen stared into the holes where her sparkling blue eyes had been replaced by holes filled with dirt and crawling insects. He couldn't look away.

Owan gasped as the stench of decay enclosed him.

'*You murdered our baby, Owen, when you murdered me. And your wife knows.*'

Lana opened her mouth, coming closer as if to kiss him.

Worms and soil dropped from her rotting split mouth and plopped onto the floor.

'*Come, Owen.*' Her face was so close. Her hand brushed his hair.

As if he was out of his body, Owen could see himself, his hand reaching out to touch her.

'No, don't.' It seemed like he was screaming in his head to stop himself from going to her because no words came out of his mouth.

'Almost there, my dear Owen. Come to me.'

The touch of her fingertips on his felt like she'd shattered his brain.

'What the hell are you doing?' an angry voice filled his head.

It was as if his body had crashed back into him. He slumped on the floor, his limbs heavy, and he couldn't move.

He felt arms pull at his shoulders.

'What are you doing, Owen? Why are you sprawled on the floor blubbering?' Freya glared at him.

He stared at Freya. 'Lana.' He finally garbled.

'Shit.' Freya shoved at him and let him go. And then, with some joy, she kicked him in the back. His squeal and his sobs made her smile.

Halfway back to the kitchen, Freya stopped. She had an unexplained urge to look back at Owen. He was still curled up in a ball.

A coldness filled the air, and Freya clutched at her arms.

The mist hovered above Owen and swirled. Freya watched in awe.

Long blond hair curled in the mist, revealing the face and sad eyes looking into hers of Lana and, for a second, Freya wanted to be in the mist.

Lana seemed to smile at her, not a monster smile, but a gentle smile.

'Freya.' A familiar voice tried to enter her thoughts.

'Freya, don't.'

The urgency in the voice broke through, and she turned to see Nathan in the kitchen doorway, his face filled with fear.

Freya turned back to look at the mist. It was gone.
Owen sobbed quietly on the floor.

Without looking back, Freya joined Nathan in the kitchen, closing the door on her crumpled husband.

After meeting Abigail and telling her about Lana and Rose, Freya now believed her husband to be a murderer.

Although she felt disappointed in herself that she'd not believed before or didn't want to believe.

The confession of Eric in the letter, telling her about the day he saw Owen murder Lana, was a hard read.

She couldn't understand why Eric hadn't intervened, but he was dead now, and Freya thought it was some justice for Lana.

What saddened Freya was Spud. He still didn't know where his mum was buried. Eric would only reveal she was on the Blyneath property.

It was like Eric wanted to control Spud to the very end.

CHAPTER 62

It was time to get the ball rolling and get Owen to confess to killing Lana.

Freya paced up and down the lounge, waiting for Owen to return from god knows where, as she knew he wasn't at work. She had phoned his workplace to get him to come back immediately, saying she wanted to talk to him to sort things out.

Headlights shone through the lounge window as Owen pulled up.

As soon as he came into the lounge, Freya couldn't help but blurt out. 'Where did you bury Lana?'.

'What?' he pushed past her and chucked his briefcase on the chair opposite the sofa.

'Why are you here? Thought you'd be off with lover boy?'

Freya stood in the lounge doorway. 'It's a simple question. Have you been drinking? You stink of whiskey.'

'Yep, it is a very simple question.' Nathan appeared in the doorway with Freya.

'Ah, there he is, lover boy to the rescue.'

'You're drunk.'

'Okay, okay, you got me,' Owen mocked them and raised his hands.

Freya watched as Owen poured himself a whiskey and plopped himself on the sofa. 'If you want one, lover boy, get it yourself.'

Nathan took a step into the lounge. He was ready to punch the smart arse. Freya held onto his arm.

'Where have you buried Lana?'

At the sound of another voice, Owen turned to find Abigail in the doorway.

'Yeah, now we have the three musketeers. Received any more texts from Lana lately, dear Abigail?'

'You bastard.' Abigail spat as she lunged at him. Owen, not expecting any physical altercation, didn't move quickly enough.

Abigail punched him square on the jaw.

His drink spilled on his shirt. 'What?'

Nathan grabbed Abigail's arm before she could swing at Owen again. 'Leave him. He's not worth it. We'll go to the police tomorrow.'

'Yeh, I'm going to the police for assault.' Owen pushed past them. 'Now, get out of my house.'

Determined, Freya asked Owen again. 'Where did you bury Lana?'

'Come on, Freya, let's not pussyfoot around him. Tell him we already know he murdered Lana and where she's buried.'

Owen turned to Abigail. 'Yeah, right.'

'Let me see. Eric was poaching in the woods when he saw you and Lana pull up in a fancy car. He heard screaming coming from the house and the next minute, you had her on the ground with your hands around her throat. Does that sound about right, you arsehole?' Abigail glared at him.

Owen laughed, a crazed, high-pitched laugh. 'Hole in one, bitch. Why do you think I bought this shitty place? Had already killed the silly girl by then. Couldn't leave her rotting in the woods, with the risk of her being discovered.'

'But out here, in the middle of nowhere, who the hell was going to find her? You could have got away with murder if you hadn't bought this place.' Nathan sniggered. 'Because since you did, they were after you. In your dreams, in your head.' Nathan tapped the side of his head.

'What?' Owen staggard to Nathan. 'Oh, lover boy speaks.'

'Yes, I do.' Nathan put an arm around Freya and pulled her closer to him.

'Get out of my house and close the damn door behind you.

Together they watched as Owen lurched across the hallway to the stairs, flopped his left hand on the handrail, and, with a grunt, heaved himself up one step at a time.

'Sleep tight, Owen.' Freya called after him.

'Yeah, yeah.' He waved at them, taking his hand off the handrail. Suddenly, he began to sway on the stairs.

'Has it got cold in here, or is it just my imagination?' Freya said as a chill breeze blew through the house.

They knew what was coming. Pity Owen Lyle didn't.

Owen struggled to regain his balance on the stairs.

The shadow hovered close to Owen. Blond hair fell down her face as she reached out and stroked his cheek. Pausing, she moved closer to him, and then her hand stroked down his chest.

'Hi, Owen.'

Owen tried to focus. His eyes fluttered as he realised who stood in front of him.

'You don't scare me anymore, you stupid bitch.'

'I've come for you, Owen. Told you we'd be together.'

With rotten fingers, a face chewed by the animals, and eyes blank, a gentle push on his chest was all it took for Owen Lyle to fall backwards down the stairs.

Owen bounced down the stairs. His screams and the crack of bones fell on deaf ears.

When Owen crashed to the bottom, crumpled, with eyes wide and now unseeing, Freya, Abigail, and Nathan just looked at each other and shrugged.

They felt nothing for the man sprawled on the floor before them. This man had deceived them all in the evilest way possible.

'Lana,' Abigail said softly as she stepped towards the shadow, her hand outstretched at the swirl of mist that played around her friend, swirling up and then down.

Lana smiled at Abigail and held her hand out to her.

Abigail reached for her hand, mesmerised by the calmness that surrounded her. A firm hand on her shoulder made her turn.

Nathan gently shook his head at her.

Abigail looked back at Lana on the stairs.

The whirl of mist had disappeared.

She was gone.

CHAPTER 63

Nathan, with Owen Lyle's crumpled body by his feet, glanced at the outhouse to see Spud appearing with two spades. He was grateful Spud agreed to help him put Owen Lyle right where he belonged.

The heavy rain had turned the ground into a bog. It would make digging the last resting place of a murderer harder.

Wet dirt, grass, and pebbles had gathered under Owen, as Nathan had dragged him round the back of the house, leaving a pathlike line toward the headstone.

'Heavy bastard.' Nathan kicked at him.

Spud's eyes met Nathan's as he handed him a spade. An understanding passed between them.

The saturated soil gave way, and in silence, Nathan and Spud dug a deep hole as Freya and Abigail held each other. They didn't want to witness what was happening but could not turn away, as if they needed to see the last of Owen Lyle dumped and buried for themselves.

'I think the hole's big enough.' Nathan dropped his spade and looked down at the dead eyes of a haunted man.

'Freya, over to you. Want to do the honours?'

With a kick and a heave, Freya rolled Owen into the hole, and as quickly as they had dug the hole, Nathan and Spud filled it in.

'Prayers, anyone?' Nathan said.

'Yeah. Rest in hell.' Abigail spat. 'Hay, look at the headstone. More letters have appeared.'

'Looks like we now know who the headstone belongs to.'

They all gathered in front of the headstone and were stunned, but not surprised, at the name.

Owen Lyle.

'Well, well, I wonder who did that?' Nathan looked at the three of them, and they all shrugged.

'We did.' A soft voice came from behind them.

Rose and Lana stood a few feet away. They looked just like themselves, fresh and alive.

'Mum,' Spud gasped and staggered to her.

'Michael. I've missed you.' she held out her hand.

Spud went to take it, but hesitating, he pulled his hand away.

'It's okay, Michael. I just wanted to tell you that you were not to blame. I didn't leave because of you. I love you.'

'Uncle Eric? Was he really my dad?'

'I'm sorry. I should have told Eric, but it was too late. Will you ever forgive me for putting you through all this pain?'

Spud couldn't help himself and burst into tears. 'Of course, ' he sobbed. Freya put her arm around him.

'Lana?' Abigail came and stood next to Spud.

'Thank you for not giving up on me, Abigail. And all of you.' 'I'm so sorry what Owen put you through, Lana.' Freya understood why Owen had fallen for Lana. She was young and beautiful.

'We can't leave you here. You need to have a respected, decent burial.'

'Don't you worry about us, all of you. Get on with your lives. We'll be fine.'

Without another word, Rose and Lana turned and, holding hands, disappeared into the darkness of the woods.

Nobody said a word for a few minutes. Not sure what they had just seen.

Spud broke the silence. 'What now?'

'Spud I ... shall we call you Michael from now on?'

Spud/Micheal beamed.

Nathan, trying not to cry, wrapped his arms around them and hugged them tight.

CHAPTER 64

Abigail shook her head in disbelief. 'I know what I saw, but don't believe what I saw. Does that make sense?' she sat on the edge of the sofa in Freya's living room. 'So, how do we deal with this? I mean, what do we tell the police? I can't tell them Lana's a ghost living in the woods. Even saying it out loud to you lot, it sounds preposterous.' Abigail looked out of the front window. 'Do you think they're in there?' She pointed at the woods. 'Watching us?'

Freya came up to her and squeezed her arm. 'I don't know, maybe. Perhaps they've seen the light and moved on, are now at peace.'

'What? You've watched too many ghost films, Freya.' Nathan teased her.

Freya turned to Nathan. 'Stop it.' she winked at him.

In the corner of the room, with Arthur on his lap, Spud quietly said. 'Lie.'

All three of them stared at him.

'What do you mean?' Freya walked over to where he sat and leaned on the back of the chair.

'Lie. Get the police off your back, Abigail, so they don't drag you in and question you. Charge you with something?' Spud shrugged.

'And tell the police what, exactly?' Abigail was intrigued by Spud's suggestion.

Over the last few days, she had come to know Spud. He was quiet and didn't speak much, but when he did, he talked a lot of sense.

She liked him. He had an air of quiet knowledge about him.

And now, now, his mind seemed at rest about his mum's disappearance. Seeing her, knowing she was okay, sort of, that she wasn't alone. Abigail noticed he now had an aura about him, a calmness, and it showed on his face. The sadness in his eyes had gone, and for the first time, Abigail saw how bright his blue eyes were.

'Tell the police Lana is safe. She just needed to get away, be on her own, after her breakup with her lying, cheating lover.' Spud said, deadpan and serious. 'No offence, Freya.'

'Non taken. Owen is … was exactly how you just described him.'

'Surely the police will want to see Lana for themselves, you know, make sure.'

Spud went and stood next to Abigail at the window and gazed out at the gently swaying trees. 'They don't know her voice, what she sounds like. Freya could pretend to be Lana.'

'That's a great idea, Spud' Nathan stood in the middle of the room, hands excitedly all over the place. 'Freya could ring the police when Abigail is there, explaining that she was Lana, that she's safe and well, that she was abroad and wanted to stay there for a while. Then Abigail could talk to 'Lana' over the phone, right there in front of the police. Confirming it is Lana. How does that sound, Spud? Is that your plan?'

Spud half-smiled at Nathan. He was beginning to like Nathan very much. In fact, he was beginning to like them all very much.

CHAPTER 65

Freya lifted the big wooden gate that led to Blyneath House and heaved it across the track so Nathan could drive the car through.

'Don't bother closing it,' he called to her once through the gate.

'I better had. That way, it'll look more secure.'

Nathan watched Freya as she closed the gate, then as she wiped her hands on her jeans as if to get rid of an unwanted filth.

She didn't move but just stood there, her arms crossed, and stared back at the house. Through the swaying trees, she could see the roof of the house. Her hair flew around her shoulders, and she shivered, even though she was wrapped up against the cold of the late afternoon.

Nathan hugged her from behind and rubbed her arms. They said nothing, just stared at the incomprehensible they were leaving behind.

'Do you think we should have just burned it to the ground?' she said, keeping her eyes ahead.

'No. We've done the right thing. If we burned the house down, there'd be police and firefighters crawling all over this place.
Let Rose and Lana have peace.'

'I guess. But what if someone comes snooping around? What if they see where Owen is buried?'

Nathan cradled her face in his hands. 'We'll be long gone by then, I'm sure. If anyone realises we're gone ...' he shrugged.
'Anyway, hopefully, the sign will put the snoopers off.'

He took her hand and led her to the car, and jumped into the driver's seat while Freya got into the seat beside him.

In the rearview mirror, Nathan noticed Abigail in the back seat, looking through the back window, with Arthur copying her.

'If I saw that sign, I don't know if it would keep me out. It would make me curious and want to go and explore, find out what was going on.'

'Look, it's Michael.' Freya tapped Nathan's arm.

'Come to see you off.' He bent and smiled at Abigail, whom he had liked from the moment he met her. He could empathise with her situation with her friend and his mum.

'Are you sure you don't want to come with us?' she asked him.

'Thanks for the offer, but, well, I'm not ready yet.'

Freya reached out to Michael and he took it in a handshake.

'Come with us.'

In a surprise move, he kissed Freya's hand. 'Thanks. But not right now.'

'Hay, Spud, you take care, okay? You've got our numbers?' Abigail stuck her head out of the back window.

He nodded.

Nathan pulled away, leaving Michael waving after them.

'I hope he's going to be okay,' said Abigail.

'He's changed a lot in the last few days. He's become strong, so I think he'll be fine. And who knows, in a few weeks, he might want to join us.'

'I'll never get used to calling him Michael.' Nathan and Abigail joined in with Freya's laughter.

Spud watched as the car disappeared around the bed and briefly wondered if he had made the right decision.

'Not much of a sign.' He grinned as he re-read the notice Nathan had tied to the gate.

'Keep Out. Risk to life. Poisonous Gases.'

CHAPTER 66

Nathan hesitated, the weight of the moment pressing upon them.

'Freya.' He whispered. 'I've been waiting so long for this moment. From the first time I saw you in the village.'

Freya snuggled into him. 'I've never been more certain of anything.'

His lips met hers in a kiss that was gentle at first and then exploratory, as if both of them were savouring the sensation of finally being free.

His kiss deepened and grew more urgent. Freya was eager to respond.

They clung to each other, lost in a world where only they existed.

Nathan lifted Freya in his arms and gently put her on the bed.

The gentle breeze from the ocean played with the lace curtains, giving the outside world a peek into their own private world.

'I love you.' Nathan whispered in her ear.

'I love you too.'

Abigail stood at the water's edge and let the warm sea lap at her toes. It made her smile that Arthur was with them as he frolicked in and out of the sea, his tongue to one side. The sea was calm, and she was relieved to think that so was she.

As soon as she, in fact, as soon as all three of them were out of sight of Hartnell, were out of sight of the county, even out of sight of the country, they all felt a welcome calmness descend upon them.

In the late afternoon, the sun still had a pleasant warmth. She held her hand against the glare.

Abigail looked back up the beach toward the villa they had rented for three months. She was sad six weeks had passed already.

She thought about Lana a lot. When they first arrived at the villa, Abigail wanted to be alone and think.

Think and wish Lana had told her right from the start about Owen Lyle. Honestly, then Lana would still be in her life. Be her best friend.

But she slowly let the questions, the what-ifs, leave her.

There was nothing she could change. Life was strange, scary, complicated, and wonderful all at once.

She sensed, no felt, deep in her heart that Lana was in a good place. In a good place with Rose.

It had taken Abigail a long time to come to this conclusion. A conclusion some people might think was ridiculous, mad even.

After all, Lana was dead. But not in Abigail's heart.

Abigail smiled and squinted into the horizon at the boats that bobbed, anchored, out to sea. Those people on the boats had not witnessed what she, Freya, Nathan and Michael had witnessed.

Lana and Rose together, for each other, forever.

She shrugged and sat down on the golden soft sand.

A voice from behind her had her turning to see if Freya and Nathan had decided to join her.

'No way.' she gasped as he approached her.

Michael waved from the top of the dune and then ran barefoot down to the beach.

'You're here.' Abigail squealed.

As soon as he reached her, he grabbed her and swung her around. 'Now why would I miss out on a freebie holiday?'

The sound of laughter filtered into their bedroom. Freya and Nathan peeked out through the curtains.

'It's Spud.' Nathan almost whooped. 'Glad he decided to come.'

'It's Michael.' Freya teased.

Holding hands, they joined Abigail and Michael on the beach.

From afar, anyone watching would think how lovely a group of friends enjoying a holiday together.

And they were friends enjoying a holiday together.

Close friends who had been through so much together had secrets that would forever bind them.

Printed in Great Britain
by Amazon

53240178R00169